A Brilliant New Novel By The Author Of *Taurus Four* And *Beyond The Sealed World*

THE DAY AFTER DOOMSDAY

Through the growing crowds at O'Hare Jetport, a tall young woman dressed like a Pan-U hostess moves, exercising the power of life or death. She rejects twenty members of an all-girl band; she chooses an aging lecturer who is planning suicide. She rejects the lovers copulating on the floor; she chooses the religious fanatic who is avidly watching them. . . .

Finally her list is complete. Those she has chosen will board the only plane to leave the jetport that day; they will escape the nuclear holocaust that is about to destroy the world. They are the ones who must rebuild civilization on

THE DAY AFTER DOOMSDAY.

Other Paperback Library Books By
Rena M. Vale

BEYOND THE SEALED WORLD

TAURUS FOUR

THE DAY AFTER DOOMSDAY

A Fantasy of Time Travel

by Rena M. Vale

PAPERBACK LIBRARY

New York

PAPERBACK LIBRARY EDITION
First Printing: November, 1970

Paperback Library is a division of Coronet Communications, Inc. Its trademark, consisting of the words "Paperback Library" accompanied by an open book, is registered in the United States Patent Office. *Coronet Communications, Inc., 315 Park Avenue South, New York, N.Y. 10010.*

With thanks to Isaac Asimov for the hint provided in "The Great Borning" in *Fantasy and Science Fiction* for September, 1967.

Rena M. Vale
1970

Prologue

The action in this account took place so many cons ago that time cannot be counted. By rare good fortune, we have a record of what happened at a certain location on the last day of the well advanced civilization that rose out of the mud of its own past and flourished for a time before destroying itself.

It is rather humbling for us to realize that ours is not the first to achieve the glory of thought, nor are we the first in manshape to crawl from slime and bestial darkness to proclaim ourselves inheritors of the Earth. But we can here resolve, with this history before us, that we will be the last; that we will allow no greed or hate to prevent us from reaching the pinnacle of our own powers. Let us then be ready, when our Sun grows dim and our planet becomes sterile, to rise in craft of our own construction to carry our culture and our creativeness to the planets of many stars, as The People in this history brought their knowledge, their courage and their creature love to ours.

Chapter I

Hugh Shipsted

A lone bird sat in a naked tree. A few desiccated leaves fluttered here and there like long-dead butterflies. The bird watched them, swiveling his little head this way and that. Silhouetted against the dark, low-hanging clouds of threatening winter, he might have been the last living thing on earth. He had gotten lost from his southbound flock, or for some obscure bird reason had decided to remain in his summer home.

Hugh Shipsted, snug in the deep foam of the Airfloat bus seat, shivered. For a moment he had felt he was that bewildered starling and had experienced the panic of utter aloneness. A sadness had always settled down on him when the leaves turned in the fall. It lingered through the gray and white winter, not to be dispelled until the first robin of spring hopped over a thawing field and the first elbow of a crocus pushed up along the garden wall. There were some compensations in winter, however—the friendly animal warmth of the cow barn when he went in to hook up the milking machines and toss fresh hay to the waiting "girls"; the rewarding spicy smell of cookies in the oven when Mother decided to spoil her only son. For thirty-eight years of his life Mother had alternately tyrannized and spoiled him. Now that she was gone—Hugh shivered again and blew his nose on an already damp handkerchief.

The bus was late, and getting later. For most of the way from Madison it had moved cautiously along the surface. When it had lifted, it had gone only high enough to clear treetops. Consequently, it couldn't gain speed enough to make up lost time. If it didn't reach O'Hare Jetport in time for him to make the Honolulu flight—He felt his shoulders shrug forward in a nervous tic, and for the hundredth time glanced at his wristwatch. He frowned scoldingly at it, shook it and held it to his ear. It rebuked his impatience with the unruffled beat of its mechanical heart. The watch, still faithful after eighty years of service, was another reminder of the departed. It had belonged to Grandfather Jensen.

Why didn't the driver—? Hugh imagined himself in the complicated cockpit of the Airfloat bus, although he had never driven one. In the position of the driver he became conscious of the shrieks and whines that tore the air above them. Everything from the mini-jets of private owners to the overseas super-jets of airlines laced the cloud-obscured sky. Other passengers in the bus were squirming, too, of which the driver became conscious. After the stop at Rockford he made an announcement.

"There's no need to be alarmed, passengers. We're having another of those tiresome emergencies—yellow alert only, but the panicky brass is trying to get everything flyable off the jetport. Schedules are all delayed a few minutes, but there have been no cancellations. We'll get you there on time. Let's all relax and enjoy the ride."

Following instructions, as Hugh always did, he tried to relax. He closed his eyes and thought of the young woman who would be his bride within forty-eight hours. His uncles didn't consider it respectful to have a wedding only two months after his mother's passing, but he felt that it was what Mother would have wanted. She wouldn't want him to be lonely. Anyway, it was better to bring the bride home in the colorful fall instead of plunging her abruptly into a Wisconsin winter, and it was too long to wait until spring. He couldn't ask Tana to postpone the wedding another six months in addition to the three years she had already waited for his affairs to settle. Now that Mother was gone—.

He shook off the recurring sorrow and forced his thoughts into the more pleasant channel of his bride-to-be. She was tall and lithe, agile as a slim fish in the water, but soft and compliant in close embrace. Tana, the mysterious and alluring, had made him forget the pressing problems at home, the quarreling uncles and his mother's failing health. Tana of the soft dark eyes, mobile mouth and mermaid body had stolen the virginity he had managed to keep through the sex-mad college years and frequent contact with hungry females in the dairy community. He was aware of his own physical appeal to women: the broad, farmer shoulders that tapered to slim waist and hips, the strong, even features, white-blond hair and girlishly pink skin. But until he met Tana on his Hawaiian vacation he had never felt the least rising interest in the females who threw themselves at him. It was as though he had been waiting for someone excitingly different. Tana, with her alien allure, was that someone.

In a flash of candor Hugh realized that he knew very little about the girl with whom he had fallen in love three years before. The high-fashion Polynesian eating house in which she worked as hostess was a long way from Hugh's Wisconsin dairy farm; the Islands of her ancestors were a long way indeed from the Norway of his forebears. Perhaps it was that differentness that lured him and had kept him enthralled through the three years of their separation. Predictably, Henry and Sibley Jensen had forbade him to bring "a naked native" to the home that was theirs only by their widowed sister's charity. (In his only picture of her, Tana wore a skin-colored bikini.) Perhaps as his mother had hinted just before her death, he had continued the infatuation out of pure Norse stubbornness, and if he should see the young woman again, he would realize his mistake.

The thought disturbed him. Suddenly he felt as if he were in a tunnel with dark gray walls pressing in on him, driving him toward a distant, impossibly small outlet. An invisible plunger was cramming him down the tapering tube, the way his mother had pressed strawberry jam through a funnel into a small-mouthed jar. Something was manipulating him in an intangible way. Hugh Shipsted, thirty-eight, one hundred eighty pounds of muscle and bone, dairy farmer of Black Earth, Wisconsin, did not accept intangibles. He struggled against the alien force while denying its existence. After a time, as though emerging into the light from a tunnel, he returned to reality. He told himself that he had dozed, as many of the fifty or more passengers in the bus were doing. The embracing foam of the reclining seats was conductive to full relaxation.

While he had dozed, someone had taken the window seat next to him. His covert glance caught the swell of breasts in profile. The new passenger was a woman with long tapered brown fingers. Her left hand manipulated a nine- or ten-inch rod, some sort of stylus, he supposed, and was making squiggles on a sheet of brownish paper fastened to a clipboard. He assumed she must have changed seats while he slept—she had not been beside him when the bus took off from Rockford, and he was sure the bus had made no stops since then. Or had it?

On the pretext of looking out the window he was able to catch a glimpse of her face. She had laid aside the stylus and was fumbling awkwardly with a lip-pencil. The movements reminded him— He caught his breath. Tana! It couldn't be! Tana was half a continent and an ocean away, waiting for him in Honolulu. He had talked to her on visaphone only the night before last about plans for their wedding. She had found a Lutheran minister, she said, just as his mother had wanted, and they were to be married in the little Combo Church where Protestants still worshipped. She had said nothing about coming to meet him of getting another job. He was sure she would have told him if she had.

The girl beside him wore a Pan-United hostess uniform. It would have been an easy matter for a hostess in a restaurant, a young and beautiful one, accustomed to handling both people and food, to get a position with an airline. Was this the surprise Tana had mentioned in a letter several weeks ago? He had concluded that the surprise was that of fulfilling his mother's deathbed wish about the church wedding. If the girl beside him was Tana, what was her purpose in meeting him this way? Was she putting him through some sort of test?

He wriggled forward in the embracing foam and sought a better look at her face. She noticed his nervous movements with a quick side glance. Her eyes, screened with long straight lashes, were liquidly brown, like Tana's. He cleared his throat and tried to make his voice sound casual.

"Looks like we'll have some snow, and here it is only October. Weather seems to be changing since they started nuclear testing again."

The girl looked up from her squiggles and flashed a red-and-white smile—lips almost too red, teeth too chalky white. Like Tana's.

"Yesth," she agreed pleasantly but impersonally, and went back to her writing.

Drained of the emotion that had surged up hotly, Hugh sank into the embrace of the seat. It couldn't be Tana. If she had come this far to meet him, she wouldn't— Or would she? He deserved to be punished for the way he had kept her dangling for three years. It was Tana's face, yet a strange face; it was Tana's lips, yet more pronounced. The small, pointed tongue that darted like an adder's between the too-white teeth, that was surely Tana's, as were the long, slender hands that were at the same time strong and yet unmarred by manual labor. The girl was left-handed, as was Tana. The more similarities he noticed, the more he doubted.

Without a warning drowsiness, he suddenly fell asleep. He didn't awaken until the driver called "All out for Pan-U."

The girl who looked like Tana had gone. Hugh Shipsted was a very puzzled man as he gathered his hand luggage and hurried off the bus.

Brock Gunnison

"There can't be a war now, can there, darling?"

Georgia Gunnison bit her lower lip to stop its trembling and went on. "There can't be a war after the agreement the President and the Premier reached last night on the hot-line. Did you hear them?"

"Ugh," came the answer from under a hat that rested over the man's face.

"You did hear them?" the woman pressed as she swung the long car onto the automatic ramp.

Brock Gunnison pushed up the hat he was unaccustomed to wearing and straightened himself in the seat. The station wagon had come to a halt on the Pan-United stop-line.

"There can't be a war, can there, darling?" Georgia repeated.

"Crissake!"

Brock crossed behind the car, lifted out his bag and bent down at the driver's window to go through the parting ritual with his wife. As he leaned down, the honey-colored spaniel, who had been scolded into submission in the back, bounded up to thrust her nose between the reaching pairs of lips.

The man flung himself away from the car. "Get that Goddamned dog out of my face!"

Jets tore the lowering clouds, a stream of them, like missiles from a multiple launch. Of the many things Brock hated, Honey the spaniel and jet-screams vied for the place of most-hated. He threw his bag on the auto-carrier as though attacking an enemy.

"Pan-U five-four-three," he snarled into the mouthpiece.

"You won't forget to call from Honolulu so Broddy and Bailey can talk on visaphone to Daddy across the Pacific. . ."

Brock didn't turn or answer. He stumbled onto the escalator, stiff with angry tension.

The station wagon bearing two-broken-hearted females moved away from the stop-line by automatic control.

Joe Quail

The centipede-jointed road truck laden with Wisconsin cabbage flashed Christmas-tree lights to signal a stop. A square man carrying a square-cornered plastic traveling bag swung out of the cab and dangled on a simiam arm until his feet touched the pedestrian belt leading to the jetport. A broad grin cracked his reddish-brown face.

"Okay—thanks." Joe Quail waved the truck on.

"Boo-enna su-erte," the Polish truck driver shouted over the roar of his engine and the shriek of jets overhead. His linguistic repertoire consisted of a few misused and mispronounced words and phrases from the language grab bags of Europe. He thought he should use his Spanish on Joe Quail.

Quail pretended he hadn't heard. He was accustomed to being mistaken for a Mexican, which was, in his opinion, an insult to an Apache-Mojave American Indian. In Hawaii he'd probably be mistaken for a Samoan, or maybe a Filipino, but that didn't matter. Good wages were paid to a man who knew how to handle a horse and a plow, both of which had come into favor in the island state since fuel-oil rationing. Also, machinery from the Mainland had priced itself out of reach of pineapple growers who had to compete with Red-bloc growers.

Joe stepped aside to let hurrying people pass him. The belt was going fast enough for him. No need to hurry, anyway. The squawking loudspeaker competing with the furious roar overhead had just announced Pan-U Flight 543 to Honolulu delayed twenty minutes more. Joe hadn't exactly heard it, but he had the faculty of understanding spoken words just beyond hearing range.

Nadine Wherry

The world's Fifth Best Dressed Woman sat rigidly behind the tiller of the tiny scooter cab. It was the "in" form of conveyance for those who traveled short distances around town where large cars were banned, or, as in this instance, from the airport hotel to flight lounges.

The bruised-petal crimson of Nadine Wherry's velvet ensemble broke away at the neckline, and out of it grew, like the pale center of a vivid flower, an enameled face that was too white, and lacquered hair that was too deeply chestnut. A glance in the mirror told her that the makeup on her brow had become creased by a frown. Without removing crimson gloves she fumbled in the crimson pouch in her lap, brought forth a stick, uncapped it and started to repair the damage. At that moment the little cab bumped to a sudden stop at the automatic Pan-United line. The door flew open; the makeup container cap rolled off her lap and onto the pavement.

"Damn, double-damn!"

Knowing that her words would be overheard by passers-by—indeed, intending that they should be—Nadine used the mildest expletive she knew.

A square brown man in a cheap synthetic suit leaped off the moving pedestrian belt and retrieved it for her.

She thanked him perfunctorily, got out of the cab and started to wrestle with the several pieces of her matched luggage—the brand Snow Advertising had made famous, and, of course, expensive. A work-calloused brown hand reached around her.

"Let me do that. You might split them pretty red britches if you lifted those bags."

Joe Quail's eyes took in the filling of the form-fitting red costume pants. Nadine moved aside to let him handle the luggage. He kept his eyes on the tightly encased posterior.

"What a nice wiggle you've got, Grandma."

Her Madison Avenue trained mind sought a withering retort, but at that moment she caught sight of a divinely tall, divinely handsome flight captain in Pan-United uniform who was moving toward her on the belt. Every line of his body was an appeal of sex, a language Nadine understood well. His eyes met hers, and she felt a magnetic pull, a hint of predestined acquaintance. She spoke to Quail without breaking the link with the flight captain.

"What nice muscles you have, Grandpa."

The Indian's merry laugh bubbled. "I see from the luggage tags that you're on the same flight I'm on—five forty-three, Honolulu. I'm Joe Quail."

Nadine's eyes followed the totem-pole figure in the Pan-United uniform. "I'm Miss Nadine Wherry, New York, Snow Advertising."

Something like an echo bounced back to her from the disappearing captain. *"Mistress* Frances Deland, pronounced *Dillon."*

Nadine snatched the remaining bag from Quail's hand. "Thank you a million. In a hurry. Just remembered a telegram I must send—to my husband!"

Joe Quail scratched his head and laughed. Something surely had ripped the old girl apart at the tight seams. It couldn't have been the thought of her husband. She wasn't the type to remember a spouse who was far away for a telegram.

Nadine made her way along the crowded corridor to the central Pan-United rotunda. Others were buffeted back, but the congealing mass of humanity was sprinkled with enough prowling males to clear a path for the woman in crimson velvet. Her waggle was inviting, and several men followed her shamelessly. Bringing up the rear of her entourage was a sun-shriveled man with a turkey-gobbler neck.

Brother Robert Smith

Robert Smith, Brethren of the Everlasting Light, had left his ranch in western Utah and set out six months before to convert the wicked cities of the East to the doctrines of the newly founded cult. His dream had receded as he found himself distracted by modern Jezebels, such as the one in red velvet who waggled her behind at him. He had been greatly relieved when the Over-priest had asked him to transfer his missionery work to one of the Hawaiian Islands where heathen lepers were said to be fornicating freely, thus spreading diseases of mind and body. He was sure his thoughts would be purified by the acid of the new work. Now he must look once more at the undulating behind in the red velvet pants.

Wide Lens

A tall Pan-United flight hostess carrying a clipboard followed Brock Gunnison into the newstand and looked over his shoulder as he twirled a rack of printed books. Nadine hurried across the waiting room. She had staked out Brock for her own pleasure on the tiresome business trip to Honolulu. He was the only one of the Snow Advertising executives with whom she had not spent a holiday, and, as she had often said, it was necessary to get acquainted with one's co-workers. Not that she particularly cared about Brock—he had been last on the list for that reason. She preferred men who were passionately wrapped up in her; Brock Gunnison was passionately wrapped up in himself. Yet his intense, hungry lovemaking had proved rather refreshing. After Honolulu, his ulcer and his Georgia could have him. Just now, however, she was not going to let the young and rather attractive flight hostess walk off with him.

Odd, Nadine reflected as she watched the girl take a stance at Brock's elbow, she looked enough like the fascinating captain to be his sister. What nationality could they be? Most of the tall people she had met on her round-the-world junkets were fair-skinned, with blond or reddish hair. Something from the Indian subcontinent, probably. She remembered seeing some very tall Sikhs in Pakistan.

She snaked her way between the hostess and Brock. He had deposited coins for a book, and it spewed out into the slot as Nadine came up beside him. She snatched it up.

"Why the reading matter? Expect to get bored?"

"Alibi. Something to be found in my pocket when I get home." Then, remembering that he and Nadine were lovers, he slipped an arm around her and drew her close. "You look like the doll you are, Tweety-Tweet."

She held a cheek to be kissed. "Make it brotherly. No telling how many of these attaché cases swinging around here belong to our clients."

The Pan-United hostess moved away, but not before Nadine again felt the mind-prickle of a censorious thought. (She *must* send that telegram to Henry to assure him that she was, as always, faithful to him.)

To cover her momentary confusion she examined the book in her hands. *"The Complete Prophecies of Nostradamus—Abridged,"* she read. "Going in for fortune-telling?"

"Didn't even notice what it was. My hand just fell on the button for it."

The tall flight hostess glanced up from the clipboard on which she was making notes in the awkward upside-down manner of left-handed writers. Her gaze locked for a moment with Brock's, although apparently he was not aware of her. Like one moving in a dream he took the book from Nadine's hand, turned the pages absently and recited without looking at the page:

> *"The eye of the object shall make such an excrescence, Because so much, and so burning shall fall the snow; The field watered shall come to decay . . ."*[1]

[1] Roberts, Henry C. (translator), *The Complete Prophecies of Nostradamus,* Century X, p. 335 (New York: Nostradamus, Inc., 1949).

He shook himself and laughed nervously. "What the hell? My ulcer's howling for some goof-oil. We've got time. Flight's delayed."

Nadine evaded his grasp and moved ahead of him into the already overflowing cocktail lounge. Her makeup enamel was creased in five or six places, giving her face the shattered look of a broken doll.

"That was a stupid thing to do, Brock." She bit off her words in angry chunks. "Any damn fool can predict the Bomb. You didn't have to make such a puking ceremony of it."

"Aw, don't make an international incident out of it."

"You ought to know what the government posters say about causing panic—the Snow Agency prepared 'em."

"You mean your pet rabbit Henry did the art work . . ."

"That's not the point. Everybody's on a hair-trigger these days. Anything can spark a panic, especially in a place like this."

"Forget it, will you? I didn't pay any attention to what I was reading—just got a notion, I guess."

"I saw the line you didn't read. It was the pay-off." She leaned toward his ear and whispered hoarsely:

"And the Primat shall succumb at Reggio."

"Ugh." Brock shook himself like a wet dog. "Earthquake there this morning. Heard about it on the radio coming in. Lot o' people killed."

"You don't have to *tell* me!" Nadine almost shrieked. "One of my dearest friends is there—or was. I'm half crazy with worry!"

Brock's lip curled, remembering what he had heard of Nadine's escapade in Italy. "Now who's starting a panic?"

She looked around quickly to see if she had attracted attention. No one could have heard her. A dozen roaming music robots plowed through the thickening crowd moaning about a *sweet bay-bee gurr-rl with a corkscrew curr-rl.* Jets screamed overhead like terrified monsters, and the amplified voice of a flight announcer droned on about postponed flights.

There were no vacant tables in the lounge, but a perplexed looking blond man in farmerish clothes sat alone at a nearby table for three toying with an empty glass. Brock pushed Nadine into one of the empty chairs and seated himself in the other.

"You don't mind, do you?"

Hugh Shipsted's troubled eyes focused momentarily on Brock's troubled face.

"Not at all. We're all in the same boat—on the same flight, that is."

Brock glanced at the blue-and-gold button on the other man's lapel which read *Pan-U 543*. "Oh . . . To be sure." He gulped back surprise and reached into a pocket.

"Forgot to put this on." He threw the flight button on the table.

Nadine took hers out of her purse and laid it beside Brock's. Both looked questioningly at the farmer.

Hugh apologized with a vague smile and unfocused eyes. "I guess I saw you at the luggage counter, or somewhere. I'm not really, not what you think. Let me buy the drinks. What'll it be?"

They mumbled their orders and sat stiffly, unsmiling, not looking at each other or at Hugh as he punched out the orders on the auto-tender. Nadine let her eyes roam and soon caught sight of the handsome flight captain standing beside the tall hostess. Both were twirling stylus-like rods, smiling and nodding, although their lips did not move. Nadine shuddered. She didn't want answers to the questions that rose like sour gorge in her mind.

The farmer, who had self-consciously introduced himself, shuddered with a nervous tic of his shoulders. He shot a quick and curious glance at the couple of twinkling rods, bit his lip and began to tremble.

Nadine assessed him. She could never endure that infantile sensitivity, the quality that appealed strongly to the maternal type of woman. He probably couldn't make love without being cosseted like an infant or a helpless lamb, but once aroused he'd be blue flame. And burn out quickly.

The Priest

The tall Pan-U hostess hugged her clipboard to her flat stomach and toyed with the wand-stylus with her other hand. Beside her a heavy-faced man with blue jowls and small frightened eyes was trying to shrink himself, turtle-like, into his too-small black overcoat. There was about him the pitiable aura of a cornered beast; he quaked and sweated and fought against the animal urge to bound away to a hiding place. The hostess, apparently taking no notice of him, pressed closer. He tried to edge away, but was halted by the hurrying stream of people who were pushing into the already overcrowded cocktail lounge. The girl moved again. This time he was helpless, and the shining tip of her stylus touched an exposed spot behind his ear. He started, then relaxed a little and shucked himself out of the heavy coat. Without a glance in his direction the hostess moved away. The man who stood trembling and exposed wore the clerical suit of a Roman Catholic priest. It was strained at every seam.

Vera Simpson and Pretty Bean

In the waiting line to the women's toilet a pregnant girl of about twenty struggled with a tangle of gear and two small children. She braced a doughy infant on her out-thrust right hip and towed a two-year-old toddler with her left hand. A purse, a diaper bag, a squawking Voicister and a lunch kit dangled from one shoulder, and a wad of wrinkled clothing in a plastic bag was thrown carelessly over the other. The long slippery bundle kept sliding down, and the girl shrugged it back, but never quite to a secure place. It was nearing the point of no return.

A gray-haired woman pushing a heavy traveling bag on the floor in front of her and shifting agonizingly from one foot to the other reached out and restored the clothes bag to the young mother's shoulder.

The girl thanked her. "Here," she offered, stepping back, "you get ahead of us. We're not in a big hurry."

The older woman's granite-like face softened. "Thank you so much. I'll do the same for you—ah, er, looks like I might have the chance, too. I see we're on the same flight to Honolulu." She indicated the flight button on the girl's handbag and displayed her own. "My name is Vera Simpson—*Miss* Vera Simpson."

"Pleasedtomeetcha. Mine's Pretty Bean—*Miss* Pretty Bean."

Vera Simpson swept a horrified glance over the infants and the swollen belly. Embarrassed, the girl tried to fill the hush. She turned up the Voicister, which was dealing with news. Another group of scientists had disappeared, and Chinese delegates had again walked out of a peace conference.

"Looks like they're going to clobber us for sure this time."

Miss Simpson gulped heftily and loosed a flow of words as though preaching to a multitude.

"We're being punished for the awful times of foul fornication and disrespect for decency. The lightning of the Lord will surely strike down those who reveled in the Sodom of the Sixties and the Seventies . . ."

"Me, you mean," Miss Bean said plaintively. "Just because I kept forgetting to take a pill."

The boy beside her set up a wail.

"Bakie!" she scolded, noticing the dribble on the floor from his loose-fitting pants. "Couldn't you wait for pottie?"

The line moved forward as several women came out of the toilet. Miss Simpson looked hopeful and inched her suitcase forward, but the door banged shut an inch from her nose. She resumed her speech.

"Like I was saying to a missionary of the Brethren of Everlasting Light who was on the Airfloat bus with me coming to the airport, the Lord has got to take people of this earth in hand. They should have a lesson they'll remember to the day of Resurrection. Brother Smith thinks so, too. He's real nice, and he's going to one of the Hawaiian Islands to work among the leprous heathen there."

The girl smiled wanly. "We're going to Honolulu to my grammother's, only I bet we don't get there. I got presumptions."

"Premonitions," Vera Simpson corrected her. At that moment she was admitted to the inner sanctum.

Evil rumor ran on whispering feet around the central rotunda and crept into the various lounges.

"It's bound to come sooner or later—looks like sooner, the way Washington and Peking squared off this morning."

"We're sitting ducks. After all the years we've had to prepare, looks like—"

"Chicago'll be hit first . . ."

"Suits me. Better'n starving or dying of fallout disease . . ."

". . . Or being eaten by them savage Reds. They say they're practicing cannibalism all over the Orient."

"Them that's left alive will all be cannibals . . ."

Against this onslaught of rumor was a wall of disbelief, the hope by which people had sustained themselves ever since Hiroshima. Civil Defense plans had been made and abandoned, bomb shelters built, stocked and left to fill with leaves and cave in. Anti-missile systems were sketched on drawing boards, ballyhooed by the world's most expensive publicists, then discarded as obsolete before they got off the drawing boards. Lethal materials sifted out of the sky, mingled with smog, affecting everything that was eaten or imbibed, but life and death went on in what was thought to be a normal manner.

Squawks from the public address system cut across the whispers.

"Arriving at Gate Two, flight number sixty-six from Paris. Repeat, Gate Two . . ."

The whispering subsided. Surely, the mob-genie reasoned, flights would not arrive from Europe if there were imminent danger in the skies.

A perspiring young man in shirt sleeves pressed a stylus to an illuminated board before him, and his handwriting, enlarged ten times, appeared on the announcement board stretched across one wall of the rotunda. Opposite the typed line "Pan-U Flight 502, Denver, 10:50 A.M.," the handwritten "Departure 11:15" was erased and the words "Departure Delayed" substituted. Flight 543, Honolulu, got the same treatment. The clerk continued down the listing with ditto marks. All departures on the board were "delayed," with no further explanation.

The Hostess

A Pan-U flight engineer looked up at the tall hostess who entered the promenade from a closed boarding area. Her eyes bored into his, and after a puzzled moment recognition lit up his face.

"Almost didn't know you in the new uniform, Anne."

The girl smiled and surreptitiously slipped her stylus up a sleeve. The engineer's eyes followed her movements.

"This time I got the sleeves long enough," she said, pulling at them. "How's Pearl?"

"She wasn't so good when I left home. Violent cramps, vomiting, like food poisoning. Don't answer the phone now." He puzzled a second. "How did you know she was sick?"

"I didn't," the hostess soothed. "I was just asking about her, but I'm terribly sorry." She said "thorry," but he didn't notice it.

"Don't you think you should go home to her?"

The engineer shrugged hopelessly. "No replacements. Everybody getting the sitting ducks out of the pond."

The hostess nodded understandingly. After a moment he went on.

"Don't think there'll be any passenger flights out of here today."

The girl he thought was Anne smiled cryptically. "I think there will be—tsomething."

The meaning of her words didn't register on the worried engineer. He stared into space as she moved away.

She slipped through the crowd, pausing here and there to glance at a flight-number button. The bulk of the crowd in the Pan-United section were passengers scheduled to go out on one of the five morning flights westward. A few early arrivals for afternoon flights east had begun to trickle in; there were some persons to meet incoming flights, and the inevitable few lost or strayed from the sections for other airlines. The mile-long plastiglas passenger building housed facilities for seven lines, and each was as jammed as the Pan-U section. However, the tall hostess gave her attention to the four hundred twenty passengers booked on Pan-United Flight 543 for Honolulu. Only a few of these caused her to bring her stylus into play, however.

Out of a package tour of eighteen, only a pensive woman who mumbled to herself attracted the hostess's attention, but after a few moments of hovering near the group, she crossed out her notes and moved on.

She stopped beside a pair of eighteen-year-old lovers who were oblivious to everything except their passion for each other. They lay across two seats and were kissing furiously and clawing at each other's clothing. The hostess moved on without making a note. She inspected a sports team of young men with orange satin uniforms emblazoned with the name of a college. They were huddled in an argument over who should pay for soft drinks. Then she stopped at an all-girl band. Twenty scrawny, sallow young women stood dejectedly clutching oddly shaped cases and studiously ignoring each other. There was a lost-looking Filipino family, a colored grandmother wrestling with five children, a pair of male lovers who were "high" on some drug. None responded favorably to some sort of test she was giving them.

Alexander Curry

A man wearing a broad-brimmed black hat and holding a mini-paper close to his eyes drew her attention. He paused a moment over an item about attempts to rescue a boy who had fallen into a well, then stopped as a prickle of hairs rose on his neck.

Another Brain Drain, the heading read. Names of a group of prominent educators who had disappeared the previous evening from the campus of the California University at Santa Cruz followed. For several months scientists, industrial leaders and educators had been disappearing singly, in pairs and in small groups of three or four. There were seven in this group. Either the unnamed Enemy was getting bolder, or the contagion of defection was spreading. Also, there was another "first" in this case. Heretofore those who had disappeared were in the "hard" sciences of warfare, the nuclear physicists, the microbiologists, the logistics engineers, and so on. This group of men and women were in the field of the so-called "soft" sciences—history, the arts, education and sociology. At the end of the list was the name of Dr. Howard McMillan, professor of religion at Northwestern University.

"Howard!" the reader exclaimed.

It had been six years since he had seen his life-long friend, and though there had been a little disagreement between them, the bond of friendship had not been broken. It was a personal loss. The reader could not understand what "They" would want of Howard McMillan; certainly he was no sympathizer or collaborator with the Enemy. The gentle philosopher and savant was more concerned with ethics, poetry and the lessons to be learned from history than with isotopes, deadly gasses and germ warfare. The reader was sure that Howard had not gone willingly. But what could be done? For the past thirty years he had been trying unsuccessfully to alert people to the dangers . . . With a sigh he passed on to the next sensation in the mini-paper.

This item pertained to the gangland execution of Nicolo (Lo-Lo) Scala who had been gunned down the night before as he was entering the residence of his harem favorite. The elegant Lo-Lo, crime boss of Chicago, had been flanked by two evening-cloaked bodyguards and further protected by an armored car full of gunmen. Nevertheless, a sniper, positioned just right in one of the high-rises across the street, had neatly and expertly planted an exploding bullet between the shoulder blades of the hoodlum boss. Police would give out no statements, but it was known that they were looking for Lo-Lo's chauffeur George (Mumble Toes) Buford, who had disappeared along with the syndicate boss's lavender Caddy.

The reader looked up from the paper to ruminate. "Lavender Caddy . . ." Then he remembered. He had seen one stop at the Pan-U entrance as he had gotten out of his cab. He tried to recall who had alighted from the Caddy, but at that moment a smartly attired heavy woman who overflowed her foundation garment rushed up to him.

The Pan-U hostess moved to one side but kept her stylus poised over the clipboard.

"You're Alexander Curry, the great lecturer!" the heavy woman gushed. "My late husband and I were enchanted, positively enthralled by the speech you gave to our club in South Bend . . ."

Curry rose and bowed in a stiff but courtly manner. He was an imposing figure, well over six feet tall and straight as a steel ruler. But there was a melancholy droop to his eyes and his wide, sensitive mouth. Shadows from the wide black hat which he now swept off accentuated the sadness of his face. His voice, trained to project, was deeply resonant, but indescribably sad.

"You're most kind, Missus Rosensmith. Such encouragement as yours is what has kept me going through all these discouraging years."

"You remembered my name!" The woman smacked her hands together and tented them coyly under her several quivering chins. "After all these busy months and all the people you must have met! You're positively clairvoyant, Mister Curry!"

"A gift," the lecturer acknowledged modestly, and looked around for an escape route.

Remembering names is the one gift I possess, he thought. *If only I could have turned it into wealth instead of wasting it on the decadent and the doomed.*

The woman was asking a question. Something about "Where to now?"

"Honolulu," he responded absently. "To visit my daughter." *And to spend the rest of my life on her charity.*

"A vacation in Hawaii! How wonderful!"

Didn't these oversize old females ever run out of expletives?

At that moment the Pan-U hostess, who had been crowded closer to him because of the rushing streams of people, stumbled against him. He steadied her.

"Musth have turned my ankle," she apologized as she pushed him away from the gushing Mrs. Rosensmith.

There had been no arrivals or departures since the plane from Paris, and the tension was mounting again in the restless crowd. Cocktail lounges disgorged an overflow; waiting room seats had all been appropriated by defiant squatters, and the row of standees who lined the walls appeared to be ready to storm the sitee section.

Children wailed; the pitch of voices rose; tempers flared.

A female screeched, "Get the hell off my foot!" and a dozen men turned, ready to do battle.

Despite the tranquillizing effect of the roaming music boxes, anxiety and hostility charged the stale air.

The overflowing woman from whom Alexander Curry was becoming separated pitched her voice over the tumult to ask, "What's the world coming to?"

The rasping tired voice coming over the public address system announced the cancellations of flight after flight "Due to uncertain weather conditions," and added, in the event someone was listening, "Passengers will be notified of flight time . . . claim your baggage without delay . . ."

No one left the rotunda. The crowd continued to thicken as *up* escalators spewed out a steady stream of people.

Sun-seekers impeded traffic with armloads of beach paraphernalia; corn-fed grandmothers clung to breeches-clad young women and slobbered over wailing infants. Swarms of teens jetted through the crowd slopping soft drinks from plasticups. Bedlam was beginning to happen.

Outside, the dark cloud mass pressed lower and lower, and a few feathers of snow tested the atmosphere like scouts for a horde of invaders.

The tall hostess questioned the tall flight captain with a look, only to receive the answer of a shrug of his shoulders. They must wait, his gesture said.

A jumping-jack man in a worn leather jacket balanced on the balls of his feet surveying the solidly packed cocktail lounge. His head was that of a hunting tomcat, tipped speculatively to one side, and his tawny tiger-eyes prowled the jungle of humanity before him. Soon they pounced on the bougainvillaea crimson of a woman's costume, and a grin of recognition split his face. He preened a moment, then lunged toward the table where Nadine, Brock, and Hugh Shipsted sat.

Grabbing the back of Hugh's chair, he shook it free of its occupant.

"Your lease has expired, buddy. The lady's expecting me."

The startled Hugh tried to protest, but the leather-jacketed man shoved him aside. A perplexed frown put another crease in the enamel on Nadine's forehead.

"Hi ya, Baby. I brought myself as a big surprise. Remember me—the Jelke party last spring?" His tone was freighted with innuendo.

Brock glared at the intruder and started to rise. Nadine pulled him back into his chair.

"You were there, Brock, dear. I'm sure you met this young man . . ." She turned to him. "Your name—it's right on the tip of my tongue."

"Hamilton, Roy Hamilton, pilot of Jelke's private plane." He thrust his right hand at Brock. "You probably remember me telling about some of my experiences in Laos—quite a party we had over there."

Brock acquiesced to a limp handshake. Indeed he did remember the man—Laosy Loudmouth, someone had aptly called him. He also remembered that Nadine and the pilot had disappeared from the party at the same time. He gulped his drink and glowered.

Nadine also remembered, and took little pains to conceal her delight over encountering Hamilton again. How could she forget the lover of six months ago who had pounced and ripped and snarled, yet had provided the ultimate in satisfaction? Nonetheless, she felt a certain loyalty to her man of the moment and tried to keep her tone on a platonic level.

"How is Rance Jelke these days?"

"I wouldn't know." Hamilton fumbled in a pocket for a coin to feed the auto-tender. He found none and looked expectantly at Brock.

The advertising executive had withdrawn into his own dark world. Nadine supplied the coin, and Hamilton punched out his order.

"You're a lifesaver, Baby. I didn't even drink my breakfast. Jelke and I had a little tiff a few weeks ago, and after he got out of the hospital—" Hamilton laughed insinuatingly and squeezed Nadine's hand.

"Managed to scrounge a ride to the Islands where I've got a real deal coming up. It'll put me in a bed of clover, Baby, four-leafed clover."

He seized the drink from the extension arm that reached from the auto-bar. "Got a lot to tell you, Baby, when we get a chance to talk." He tossed the drink down his gullet and reached his hand for another coin. Nadine supplied it with a glance of "What-else-can-I-do?" at Brock.

"Matter of fact," Hamilton continued, "we might be able to cut you in on the deal. We'll need a smart woman operator." He coughed and leaned closer to Nadine.

"How 'bout loaning me a couple more iron men so I can get a little package o' lunch to take along?"

"You can't take liquor on the plane," Brock cut in sulkily.

"Don't you ever think Roy Hamilton can't, buddy. I've got more angles than you ad-men ever thought up. I can—"

Nadine shoved the coins into the pilot's hand and indicated a vendor against the wall.

"We'll get together later, Roy. Brock and I have some things to discuss now, haven't we, dear?"

Hamilton leaped up like a jack-in-the-box. "If that's the way you want it, Baby!"

Nadine moved her chair closer to Brock's. He leaned away from her.

"You don't have to make any sacrifices on my account."

"Brock, darling, you know there was nothing else I could do."

"You're not going to make it."

The toad-like Dorf Allman wriggled and stuffed her three-hundred-pound bulk into the bucket seat behind the wheel. The mini-car, which had stopped on the Pan-United line, creaked and groaned.

"You hope I won't!"

Dorf's companion, a thin, ungainly woman in a scruffy fur coat, eluded the oversized paw that clutched at her.

"Is that the only goodbye I get?"

"Not here, Dorf," the thin woman scolded. "I'll write you."

"Ella, Ella," the fat woman pleaded, the putty of her face sagging into porcine lines, "don't leave me. I've got nothing . . ."

"The car," Ella argued, not coming within reach of the outstretched hand. "I'm giving it to you. Signed over the ownership card—it's in the dash compartment. Hope it won't give you any trouble." She turned away.

The fat woman made a last try before the car was nudged forward by the automatic guide.

"Don't fail to contact the Daughters when you get to Honolulu."

"Daughters!" Ella scoffed to herself as she skipped toward the escalator. "Hereafter, it's the *sons* for me—if they'll look at me."

It was fortunate, she reflected, that she had been foresighted enough to check her luggage at the Grand Street terminal before calling for Dorf. She had been correct in assuming that the toad-woman, who had tried every ruse to prevent her from leaving, would keep her waiting in order to make her miss her flight. They had been in a tug of war for six months as Ella had tried to break away from The Daughters. She had not told Dorf about the teaching contract she had signed to tape lectures on modern art in Honolulu, and Dorf had assumed that she would be dependent on what they euphemistically called "our people" to find her a position.

By the time Ella reached the rotunda, doubts began to nag her. She sought assurance from the lighted announcement board. Flight 543 was still postponed! Her troubled mind screened out the ditto marks that traced down from the word *indefinitely*. Before long, however, she reacted to the contagion of fright and anxiety that rose like a miasma from the close-packed crowd in the rotunda. She felt old, lonely, desperate.

She repeated a slogan she had learned long ago: "Love is a thing to be shared." It did not bolster her spirits. There was no one in this boiling crowd to offer or to receive love. She grieved sympathetically over the heartbreaks, the fears, and the little sorrows of those around her. She gave, but there was no one to tune in, much less return her offering. Her eyes momentarily met those of a tall, dark flight hostess, and she felt a nudge of something, but it was not the love she had learned to identify.

Then she caught sight of the priest. A lump rose in her throat, and she fingered the gold cross which dangled from a neck chain. An urge she could not understand drove her forward.

"Father!" she sobbed as she reached the man in priest's garb. "I'm a miserable sinner, and I have no confessor. Will you—"

She sank to her knees and clutched at the rough hand that dangled below a sleeve that was too short. Her lips sought a ring, but finding none she kissed the knobby knuckles.

"Forgive me, Father . . ."

"Don't take it so hard, lady. I mean, bless you, my child." He withdrew his hand and backed away.

When Ella looked up he had disappeared. She crossed herself and rose to her feet where she swayed, overcome with her utter aloneness. She might have fallen if a Pan-U hostess hadn't supported her.

"Are you all right now, Misth?"

"Pozniak," Ella supplied, then colored in embarrassment when she realized the young woman was not asking her name. She was alone again.

Alexander Curry, now steeped in the gloom of self-pity, searched his pockets and drew forth a small cloisonné container which had been his great-grandfather's snuffbox. However, the scent which wafted from it when he opened it was not that of old tobacco. It was the almondy smell which identified the black-market item known as the Pill of Last Resort. Curry looked around for a drinking fountain, spotted one and started toward it carrying the Pill ready to pop into his mouth.

Someone rocketed into him, jarring the precious Pill from his hand and sending it skittering into the path of a hundred tramping feet.

"Tso tsorry."

The apology came from the tall Pan-U hostess with the clipboard. There was something about the girl's red-and-white smile that made him forget his macabre errand.

"It's all right," he assured her, surprised that he meant it.

Brother Smith had often watched his goats mating, but never before had he seen humans going through the antics of unfastening clothing, kissing each other's bodies and squirming together on the floor. Several times he had passed the seats where these lovers pawed each other intimately, and each time he had told himself that they were possessed of the devil and that he must shun them until the Evil One lessened his hold on their souls. But each time he found himself returning to the spot. Now they were brazenly copulating on the waiting room floor and he couldn't unglue his eyes from them.

Some of the passersby pretended not to notice them; others gave them a scornful glance and hurried on. A few gawked openly, and several teens crowded up to shout obscenities at them. Brother Smith's face grew beet-red, and a fast pulse throbbed in his throat. Unknown to those around him, the pure-in-heart Brother Smith was going through an experience of his own.

Osta Eisen

The wheezy old surface bus which brought Osta and Elsbeth from the festering heart of the city was late. If the flights around eleven hours had not been postponed, they would not have arrived in time. The bus passengers had been informed of delayed schedules, but Osta was not the trusting type. When the vehicle reached the Pan-U entrance the energetic Mistress Eisen lost no time in getting out the door. She jerked the hand of her seven-year-old granddaughter so vigorously the child's neck almost snapped.

"You got lead in your feet like in your tokus?" the woman demanded, her scolding voice softened with love. "We've got to hurry, or we'll not see your Mommie in Honolulu."

"I'm hurrying, *Grossmutter,*" the little girl whined, "only my hurry is not so fast as yours."

"Shut up and talk English," the grandmother admonished. "Born in this country you were, and so was your mother, and you speak yet like you were just over here from the Old Country."

While she talked, Osta was trotting toward the luggage compartment where the driver was struggling with a mountain of bags. She plunged in like a dog diving into a rabbit hole, burrowed in the pile a moment and emerged, disheveled, carrying three bags. She shoved one at her granddaughter.

"The littlest one for you, Elsbeth."

The girl staggered, barely able to lift it.

While the driver and other passengers stared aghast, the gray-haired woman tossed the largest bag to her left shoulder, balanced it there with an arm from which dangled purse, knitting bag, lunch kit and one or two other sundry items. Then she picked up the other bag, and in the crook of that arm scooped up Elsbeth, who clung tightly to the "littlest" bag. Thus loaded and festooned, the block-built woman trotted rapidly to the escalator and mounted the moving stairs two steps at a time.

Watchers shook their heads in disbelief.

The driver turned back to the other passengers, who were waiting for their own bags. "They don't make 'em like that any more," he observed laconically.

Still carrying the assortment of luggage and the half-strangled child, Osta bulldozed her way through the crowd in the rotunda to the weighing station. Effortlessly she tossed the bags on the moving belt and punched out her destination and flight number. The belt stopped.

"Deposit seven dollars and sixty-four cents overweight charge, madam," the tired clerk intoned.

"Overweight?" Osta shouted, blowing a straggle of hair from her eyes. "What do you mean, overweight? Everyt'ing I weight yet on my own scales at home."

Her voice, harsh and masculine, overrode the competing noises, inside and out. Conversations ceased and heads turned, many welcoming the distraction.

The child, conscious of the spectacle her grandmother was making, tugged at Osta's billowing pantaloons.

"Grandmother, I've got some money . . ."

Osta pushed her way. "I don't need your money. All I need is for this man to get some sense."

"Please, madam, you must deposit—"

"Don't tell me again. I'm not deaf. See, big ears I've got." She reached up and flapped ears which were somewhat oversize.

"Your scales are wrong, *crooket,*" she bellowed. "A nice way to make a little extra for yourself. Not one dime of my money do you get!"

On the other side of the rotunda the tall hostess and the tall flight captain exchanged glances, and their rods twinkled. He nodded and made his way toward the weighing station. When he reached it, Osta was still shouting invective at the harried clerk while she drew bone hairpins from her disarrayed hair.

The flight captain's darting eyes appraised the woman's rough-hewn, square shoulders, the rectangular face and the eyes, not unlike his own, in which there were misty depths.

"I am the captain of your flight, Mistress Eisen," he was heard to say. "Can I be of any help to you?"

His eyes sought hers, and she flashed back a look which grappled with his. Their gazes locked like the arms of evenly matched wrestlers, and thus the young man and the older woman remained rigidly immobile for thirty or forty seconds.

Osta was first to move. Strangely subdued, she stuffed hairpins into her mouth, drew money from her purse and shoved it at the clerk. That puzzled young man punched the button which released the belt to move the controversial bags out of sight. With her eyes still locked on those of the flight captain, Osta took the pins from her mouth one by one and placed them carefully in the braids that wrapped her head. When the last pin was in place, she replied to his question. Her voice was husky with emotion.

"Yes," she said. "I am."

A faint smile flickered on the captain's stony face, and he turned away. The awed crowd fell back to clear a path for him. There were a few nervous giggles here and there, and a scoffing "Aw" or two, but for the most part those who had witnessed the incident at the weighing station were silent.

Osta trailed meekly after the tall captain, and Elsbeth, apparently forgotten, trotted behind her grandmother. They disappeared through a door that was lettered "For Flight Personnel Only."

The tall hostess fell in behind them and closed the swing door so gently it gave no sign of having been opened.

Chapter II

Static and background noises blurred the announcements over loudspeakers, but a tired voice droned on with patient determination:

"Flight five, five, four, repeat, Flight five fifty-four, canceled. Passengers will be notified of departure time. Flight five, four, eight, repeat, five forty-eight, canceled. Passengers must leave phone numbers where they can be reached. Do not call us; we will call you. Cards are at all flight counters; fill out and leave them in containers provided. We repeat, do not call us; we will call you. Baggage will be returned downstairs. Claim it immediately, please. We will not be responsible . . ."

Another voice came on, not from the communications speakers, but from all around, like a voice from the sky. It was musically feminine, rippling water over stones, and a slight lisping accent gave it an exotic quality.

"Passengers of Flight five, four, three, repeat, five forty-three, attention. Will the following persons report immediately at Gate Twenty, repeat, Gate two-oh:

"Mister Hugh Shipsted;
Mistress Frances Nadine Wherry Deland;
Mister Brock Gunnison;
Mister Joe Quail;
Miss Pretty Bean and two infants;
Mister Alexander Curry;
Father Martin O'Banion;
Mister Roy Hamilton;
Miss Ella Pozniak; and
Brother Robert Smith.

"Report at once to Gate Twenty. It is urgent. Thank you."

The tired voice continued over the speakers. "Flight five, eight, one, repeat, five eighty-one . . ."

Vera Simpson banged her suitcase against the back of Brother Smith's knees. Startled, he turned from the pair on the floor who had thumped to a climax and now lay in each other's arms like limp rags.

"Didn't you hear your name called?" Vera panted. "They must have called my name, too, but I didn't hear it. We're on the same flight. Gate Twenty—we must hurry."

Smith twisted his turkey-like neck around without moving his body.

"Don't know what they're thinking of, letting the goats come in here and run all over the place." His eyes were cobwebby and unfocused.

"There are no goats, Brother Smith," Vera said patiently. "I guess it's just the strain we've all been under this past hour and a half. But it's over now. Our flight has been called. Come on."

He shook his head, his Adam's apple bobbing up and down along his thin neck. His eyes cleared as he blinked away the cobwebs.

"Flight's been called? You mean—?"

"We're off to Honolulu, Brother Smith, God willing."

"Er, yes, God willing." He smiled at her, reddened and reached down to take her suitcase.

Brock found himself on the moving walkway with Hugh Shipsted. Hamilton had appropriated Nadine and was telling her something about "a sweet little deal." Outside, it had begun to snow in earnest; large, wet flakes plastered themselves stickily on the plastiglas along the walkway, giving the passage the aspect of a tunnel.

Hugh's shoulders twitched in a nervous tic and he laughed deprecatingly.

"Always seem to be going through a tunnel."

Brock gave no indication of having heard.

"They should have canceled it," he mumbled sullenly. "Not safe flying in weather like this, no matter what their blinking instruments say."

Ella Pozniak, taking long, mannish strides, pushed around them trying to overtake the priest, who hurried, head down, in front of them.

"I can see it now," she declaimed, "the city sparkling with lights, Diamond Head crouched like a long black lion before the curtain of mauve sky . . ."

"Yus, er, God bless you, my child," the man in cloth muttered, and stood aside to let Ella pass him.

Alexander Curry stared ruefully at the scattered crystals of the pill he had carried for more than a decade. For years he had publicly predicted The Worst—anarchy, savagery, the downfall of the nation and the coming of a new slavery system. The Pill of Last Resort had been his insurance against being captured alive by the forces of evil. Now that it was crushed, he began to doubt his own predictions. The flight was going out. His name had been called. He looked around for the belt to Gate Twenty.

Joe Quail picked up the little boy who the young mother was pulling like a sled behind her. The child had missed his footing and was bouncing along on his stomach, too winded to cry out.

"Don't you think it's funny that no more people on our flight were called?" the girl asked when Quail came alongside her.

The Indian shrugged. "Maybe everybody else is aboard—we didn't hear the flight called, or something." He knew that wasn't the case, but he hated to see the young mother get all stirred up. It would sour her milk.

"I don't think he's really a Catholic priest," Vera Simpson whispered to Brother Smith.

"Who?"

"That man bundled up in the black overcoat."

"He's got on a priest's clothes."

"Maybe he was a ragged tramp and the priest gave him something to wear."

Alexander Curry, not content to passively ride the moving walkway, swung alongside to hear Brother Smith's remark.

"Ragged tramps seldom ride in lavender Caddies."

Brother Smith goggled. "Him? How do you know?"

"The Caddy was just ahead of my cab at the Pan-U entrance. I saw him get out of it."

"They've got a lot of rich parishioners in that faith," Brother Smith sniffed enviously.

Vera Simpson also sniffed, but with more emphasis. She knew a bad thing when she saw it.

Standing beside the entrance to an old-fashioned gate leading to the open field was the totem-pole flight captain and a smaller, darker man who might have been built of carefully graded boxes. Laughter lines were deep around his mouth, and his eyes twinkled almost as brightly as the rod he held in his hand. Both men were toying with stylus rods, or swagger sticks tipped with a silvery substance. The rods twinkled as the men gestured to each other.

When the small group of passengers came up, the captain spoke in slightly accented but precise English.

"We have been granted special permission to take a few of you from Flight five four three in an executive jet which we are ferrying to Honolulu. Other passengers for the flight will follow on the regular plane. Your baggage has been taken aboard, and we will endeavor to make you as comfortable as you would be on the large skyliner. There is one request we must make . . ."

He paused to consult silently with his companion. The shorter man gestured, the captain nodded and stepped back. The second man held up his rod to catch attention, and his voice was less strained than that of the captain.

"The plane we are taking is equipped with a new type of power plant—fully tested and proven to be reliable. However, the presence within a short radius of this engine of electronic devices may cause some trouble. Therefore, Voicisters, transistor timepieces, and other such devices must not be taken aboard. The valuables will be sent to your destination on the skyliner, and you may claim them at the other end of the flight. We assure you that every care will be taken of your property, and we hope you will suffer no inconvenience."

He indicated a strangely shaped earthenware vessel with a long and gracefully curved neck. It was decorated with what appeared to be an Aztec design of four joined heads with eyes that looked almost alive. The eyes watched the four points of the compass and gave one the feeling that they would miss nothing.

The speaker bestowed a broad smile on Pretty Bean and continued; "Those dependent on timepieces to regulate infant feeding, or for the purposes of medication, can learn time from our stewardess, who will always be ready to help in any way she can . . ."

Hamilton, more than a little drunk, elbowed his way forward.

"Le'ss get on with it, shall we? I want to get a good look at the Skylark, or whatever the narky crate is."

He thrust his right hand under the captain's nose. "Roy Hamilton is the name, Lieutenant Be-Jeezez Roy Hamilton, the boy who put the fly in the Brown Babies' ointment in Laos. Were you in on that li'l operation?"

The startled captain staggered backward, and the shorter man reached over to take Hamilton's hand.

"Bennett is my name, Lieutenant Hamilton. I'm the engineer on this flight. Garner, here, is the test pilot from the factory. Would you please leave your watch in the receptacle, then I'll show you around while the others are boarding."

Hamilton laughed loudly and spoke behind a hand. "Uncle Moe got my watch and a few other li'l items last week . . . You know."

The engineer nodded sympathetically. "I understand. This way, Lieutenant."

He pushed open the plastiglas door, which had become caked with snow. As they stepped through, he touched the tip of his stick to the back of Hamilton's neck. The flyer staggered, and Bennett supported him.

Nadine did not strip off her watch as others did. She looked up pleadingly at the captain.

"Surely this little thing couldn't make any difference with your gears or whatever. It cost me a fortune to have it made to my specifications in Switzerland. All these little tiny rubies on the hands are perfectly matched. I could never get it replaced . . ." Her hair brushed the tall captain's cheek as she held up the watch.

Garner surreptitiously pushed away the harsh hair but bestowed an intimate smile on the enameled-faced woman. He touched her shoulder with his swagger stick.

"You need have no fear, my dear lady. Anything is safe in the stomach of the *ginga.*" He touched the swan-necked vessel with his stick, and meekly Nadine fed her watch into it.

Pretty Bean had trouble getting the Voicister strap untangled from others over her shoulder, and Vera Simpson stepped forward to help her.

The captain pointed his stick at Miss Simpson.

"Your pardon, madam, but your name was not called."

Not in vain had Vera Simpson battled her way through thousands of slum rent collections. Seldom had she needed anything more formidable than an outthrust jaw. She now thrust out her jaw.

"If this is Brother Smith's flight, it's my flight, Captain Garner, and I'm taking it."

"I'm sorry, please, but the luggage for only those whose names were called was taken aboard this plane. It would—"

Miss Simpson made it a practice never to let adversaries finish what they had to say.

"That's just where you've been outsmarted, *Mister* Garner." She snatched the bag from Brother Smith's hand and heaved it to the top of the turnstile gate. "I never trust my belongings to the indifferent care of an automated machine. Now, *if* you please . . ."

Garner regarded her fixedly for a moment, then touched her arm lightly with his wand-rod.

"Step aside, please. Let the others pass."

She slapped the rod away from her arm. "I'm not being shoved aside!"

The captain bowed and smiled but did not release the turnstile for her. "There are formalities, dear lady. I must have your ticket and must inspect your travel papers."

She allowed herself to be thrust aside, but waited with a glitter of suspicion in her eyes.

Hugh Shipsted paused at the receptacle where Curry, the priest and Brother Smith had deposited their watches. He fumbled with the strap of his grandfather's wristwatch.

The flight captain glanced at it, held his rod before Hugh's face and shook it. Although Hugh appeared not to notice the shining object, he refastened the watch strap. Deliberately, he took gloves from a pocket, drew them on carefully and turned up the collar of his overcoat. At the door he turned, shielding his face from the driving snow, and spoke as though imparting a gem of profound sagacity.

"Looks like we're in for some snow. It's unseasonably early this year."

Chapter III

Tears oozed from under Osta Eisen's swollen eyelids and felt their way down her craggy face. Why, she asked herself in the near-delirium of torment, had she allowed anyone to open the door into the secret cellar of her life? It had been closed and locked since the disappearance of *Mutter* so long ago in the Sudenten section of The East. Gerda Mayer, beloved mother, fair as a Nordic, fragile as translucent china, had arranged a get-away passage to *Amerika* for her ugly foundling daughter, and when the fourteen-year-old girl was known to be safe at her uncle's farm west of Chicago, Gerda Mayer disappeared. Disappearances were not unusual in that newly communized country, and the family in America assumed that she had been arrested and taken away.

Maybe, Osta speculated, *Mutter* had somehow managed to live; somehow she had managed to send word to her strange-born child, whose rugged features were undoubtedly those of an Eastern savage in the occupying army who had raped the small, delicate German girl. Osta did some mental calculations and concluded that the tall young man with the wood-block shoulders and magnetic eyes could be a younger brother. He was surely the son of the father whom she had been left to imagine. No doubt he had been told of the foundling from Germany and had set out to find her. Else why would he have asked in the whirly thoughts that were driven into her mind by the electric current from his eyes, *"Are you the daughter of Gerda Mayer?"*

He had spoken aloud to shield the mind-to-mind communication, but she hadn't even heard the oral question. With his mind reaching out, probing into the memories in the locked part of her mind, how else could she have answered except to say, *"Yes, I am."*

"Grossmutter!"

Osta opened her eyes on the neglected little blonde girl who clutched at her. "How many times must I tell you that to speak German is *verboten?"*

"I'm sorry, Grandmama, but I am hungry and I must go to bat'room and we are flying high above the clouds."

"There is plenty food in the lunch box I brought—homemade *brot* from wholesome hand-harvested, stone-ground flour, and some home-cured meat and home-canned pickles. And you know how to find your way to the washroom—you've been on airplanes before." She picked up the knitting she had dropped when she had succumbed to thought.

"This one is different, Grandmother," Elsbeth whimpered. "It do not have the lit-up sign, and not regular seats in rows. The windows are high up—I had to stand on the bed-thing to see out—and the floor is like spongy grass."

Osta looked around and for the first time since she had boarded, saw the conventional interior of a small plane. It was luxurious, with a thick green carpet underfoot and damask-covered reclining chairs for seats. She remembered that the flight captain had said when he conducted her inside that it was a special private plane that would take them to their destination more quickly than the big sky-liner. She had been too shocked and confused to observe her surroundings before, but now she took in the green-gold color scheme, the circular cabin with small, porthole windows and adjustable contour seats fanned around so that passengers reclined like swimmers in a water ballet wheel. But where was the sign that meant lavatory or toilet, or whatever the rich owner had decided to call it?

"Let me show her the way."

The tall hostess, who also acted as stewardess on the small plane, reached a hand down to the little girl.

Osta took a thick, dark sandwich from the lunch kit extracted a bottle of home-canned apple juice and hel them ready for her granddaughter. She had no appetite For the first time she noticed the other passengers wh were sunk down into the deep foam of the reclining seats Most of them appeared to be dozing or just relaxing, a except the beady-eyed thug in the priest's suit who wa sitting up stiffly holding a gold-lettered missal before h face. Osta knew that he was not Father Martin O'Banio of St. Serafino's Church, as he kept telling himself ove and over that he was. She didn't know, or care, who h was. Always people pretending to be something or some one they were not, like that woman with the dyed ha and enameled face, pretending she was a *Miss* when all t time she was married to one man and sleeping with an body else who asked her. Osta wondered idly what these people had to do with the private business betwe her and her mother. Or was it her father to whom she w being taken?

Brock's ulcer throbbed, his head ached, and he hat himself. He couldn't imagine why he had arranged a l tryst in Honolulu with the wife of the mousy little direc of the Art Department. Maybe after all these years in the advertising business the glamor of Madison Avenue had gotten to him, in spite of his pretended preference for the Old Hog Butcher of the West and insistence on remaining in the Chicago office. But Georgia had gotten on his nerves lately; she didn't have to be so damned passionately suburbanite with an antiquated station wagon and a watchdog and dancing lessons for the kids. Dancing lessons for boys! No wonder a third of the males in the country were homosexuals!

He glanced at the woman half hidden in the foam-rest seat beside him. She certainly wasn't beautiful; her face had the glazed look of the third lift job, and her voice was strickly martinis-on-the-rocks. Her hair was harsh from dye, and her tattooed lips were swollen and stiff. Yet he had to admit it did something to his maleness to kiss those lips, especially when she plied the false eyelashes on his cheek. She wasn't young—upper forties at best—but her figure was Willowanda's best, with a touch of foam rubber on the upper structure and an aphrodisiac curve behind. The way she could waggle that cushioning really stirred up sleeping glands! But why did she have to disgrace him by carrying on with that Laosy pilot? That's what had burned his ulcer. He belched and spit bloody foam into a handkerchief.

The priest on the other side of him, who had his nose buried in a prayerbook, looked up, noticed the blood and placed a hand on Brock's knee.

"Dake it easy, son. Goat's milk best t'ing in the world for an ulcer. I cured mine that way."

Sickened at the thought, Brock squirmed away. "Thanks, Father."

"God bless you, son." The priest lifted the prayerbook before his face again.

Warmth and quietude washed over Brock. The priest's words had had a tranquillizing effect. Certainly goat's milk was preferable to the gooey kind of religion Georgia's priest was always trying to shove down his throat. The "son" was a nice touch, too. Long time since he'd been called *son*. And he'd never known a man he could sincerely call *Father*. No wonder he had an ulcer, after all the stepfathers he had had while he was growing up.

Nadine stirred and extended a claw-fingered hand toward him. "Ulcer howling again, darling?"

"Nev' mind," he growled.

"Don't be like that, Brock, dear. I couldn't help it that my old friend Roy Hamilton spun in on us that way. I just couldn't brush him—he might have made a scene. But you should know me well enough to know I'm always faithful to the man I'm with. I'm yours, Brock, and only yours, for a lovely long weekend."

"Ugh." It was better to be noncommittal, he decided. He looked around and discovered that the Lieutenant of the Laotian War was stretched across two seats snoring drunkenly.

Nadine was hurt. Her underlip quivered, and the hand that lifted a glaze-repair stick to her face trembled. Brock was sorry he had been gruff.

"Nice little sky-car, this," he offered pleasantly. "Probably being delivered to some pineapple king."

"It's Rance Jelke's castoff plaything. Don't you remember the Agency ordered those irridescent bombazine drapes made up in India specially for him?"

"That was bluish-green stuff. I remember it."

Nadine looked around. "Just what would you call this?"

"Tangerine and brownish green. And don't tell me it's the light. I got a good look at it when we came aboard and the door was dropped down."

Nadine laughed indulgently and Brock turned away from her. The woman was going over the borderline. Just because she'd had a love tryst in the Jelke plane, she imagined this one was just like it! He closed his eyes and gave himself up to the contemplation of his visceral debilities. He shouldn't have taken that drink. It was cauterizing his ulcer with fire. He was conscious of the hostess hovering over him, and he waved her away.

"Couldn't think of food right now."

"Try this, please, Misther Gunnison."

She held out a glass of creamy-looking milk. It was obviously not the "syn" stuff one got in paper containers from an automat, and he noticed that it gave off a musky aroma. Before he could frame a question, the turkey neck of Brother Smith swiveled around.

"Goat's milk!" the missionary crowed.

Brock reached for it. By the time the first swallow reached his stomach, his ulcer had stopped throbbing.

"Tea, coffee or syn-milk, Mistress Dillon?"

Nadine opened one eye and stared up suspiciously at the brown-faced girl who hovered over her.

"How could you know that's the correct pronunciation of my husband's name? You pronounced it *De-land* before."

The girl drew away. "It was a mistake," she said thinly. "Please pardon."

Nadine sat up and worked the other eye open. The gummy makeup on the false lashes had locked it shut.

"It's a mistake to call me De-land or Dillon. That's my husband's name—not mine. My name is Wherry, *Miss* Nadine Wherry."

"Yesth, Misth Nadine Wherry... Would you like tea, coffee—"

"*No* food, if you please. How do you think I keep my figure?"

The girl refrained from answering and withdrew quietly.

Nadine felt better. It gave her a feeling of superiority to put a service person in place. She looked around at the other passengers, all of whose faces were visible because of the seating arrangement which Rance Jelke had called *companionable,* with seats ranged around as in a living room. The morose man who had put aside his black planter's hat was too old to be interesting; Joe Quail was some sort of native who might suffice for a quickie affair if he could be torn away from those puling brats. The man with the turkey-gobbler neck wasn't even an interesting animal.

Nadine hardly ever allowed herself to remember the Iowa farm where she had been Frances Wherry, but the turkey-necked man brought it back, with the stinks of the henroost and the pig pen and manure on the corn rows warming in the spring sunshine—ugh!

Roy Hamilton stirred, and she tried to catch his eye. At that moment the stewardess approached him with a tray.

"You should eat some-ding, Misther Hamilton."

Hamilton awakened with a roar. "Eat something? Damned right. I'd like to take a bite out of your behind, Baby! Come over here, let's get chummy."

The girl evaded his clumsily groping paw and set the tray in front of Hugh Shipsted.

Hugh quickly swung around the empty seat between him and Hamilton so that it blocked the pilot's move toward the stewardess. After a few futile attempts, Hamilton subsided into instant sleep.

Hugh looked up at the girl with pleading spaniel eyes. "Sit here beside me, dearest Tana."

He hadn't meant to speak to her before she formally recognized him, but as he watched her every move he became convinced that she was waiting for him to speak.

"Misther Shipsted, you musth not call me by a name that belongs to another."

Hugh jabbed at the food, which was strange to him. Everything had gone out of focus, or he'd been shoved into a fun-house with a lot of crazy mirrors. He wanted to be a little boy again so he could ask his mother to fix what was wrong.

"Why shouldn't I call you Tana when you are Tana?" He felt his lip tremble.

The young woman bent over him solicitously. "Everything is very confusing, is it not, Hugh Shipsted? Your innocence I love. But, please, *Tana* is the word in my language for refuse—what you say, garbage."

Hugh melted. "I don't care what your name means, my dear. I didn't realize how much I love you until I've seen you again." He laid a hand tenderly over one of hers.

She placed her other hand over his. "Have it as you wish, Hugh Shipsted of Black Earth. Sleep now, the sleep of the little child that you are."

Obediently, he nodded, and she took the tray of barely touched food from him.

Vera Simpson shifted the topheavy bulk of her superstructure onto the edge of Brother Smith's seat-rest.

"You ask me," she whispered juicily in his ear, "that's the reason for our special flight. The hostess wanted a nice, cozy trip with her lover."

"Trip?" The scrawny neck elongated as Brother Smith's sleep-towsled head shot up. "Dangerous, hostess taking a trip while we're in flight. Must speak to the steward about that."

Vera shifted back to her own seat. "I didn't mean that kind of 'trip,' Brother Smith—nothing about drugs. I meant that the lovers wanted to be together and that they arranged for this small, cozy plane."

"Lovers, you say? Where?" Smith swiveled his head around, his eyes pruriently seeking a sight such as he had witnessed at the jetport.

Vera sighed. "I didn't mean they were— Look, you're tired, Brother Smith. Best you go back to sleep." She knew he was a good man, but sometimes the good ones were worse than the bad ones.

Odd, she mused, how everyone seemed so drowsy. Even herself, and she was generally regarded as an exceptionally wide-awake person. There was something most peculiar about this flight. It wasn't a Communist kidnapping, certainly. There didn't appear to be any Big Brains here, or anyone who would be worth a ransom. It didn't make sense. Did anything in this sodomistic world make sense?

Take this luxurious sky yacht, for instance, with its whirly-gig orange and yellow decorations, wild-cherry-colored carpet and tiny, high-up windows? Why would anyone want to spend good money on a stomach-turning thing like this? Yea, verily, as Brother Smith had remarked, the wicked world needed a lesson in fire and flood.

Ella accepted the tray of unappetizing food because she didn't know how to refuse. She wasn't hungry and didn't feel as if she ever would be. Gingerly she picked at a gluey mass that might have been a mixture of tapioca, carrots and syn-meat.

"Don't eat that old sawdust food!"

For the first time Ella noticed the woman beside her—foreign-looking, with black snakes of hair wound around her head, dark eyes with misty depths in them and facial boning that was positively primitive. A portrait of her would be mistaken for a cartoon. A hand that was too broad and calloused to be feminine held out a huge untrimmed sandwich.

"Organically grown, hand-harvested, stone-ground, home-baked . . ."

Ella remembered a news picture she had seen on the TV a few weeks previous. It was of the same woman who was speaking to her. She accepted the sandwich.

"You're the woman in the Danish home bakery."

"Bohemian," Osta Eisen corrected her. "The rat poison was only in the boughten flour—that stuff's all doped up, anyway. My husband made a mistake, that's all."

"He died, didn't he?" Ella realized that sounded crude, and she hastened to soften the statement. "By mistake, I mean. It was on the news and in the mini-papers."

"Mistake, yes."

The older woman returned to her knitting and began to count stitches. "I got three grandchildren to make pull-overs for and this is only number two." She counted again, dismissing Ella.

The sandwich was tasty, but Ella could choke down only a few bites. She dropped the remains on the food tray and covered them with the paper napkin. There was a hollowness inside her, and it was expanding like a balloon that was being blown up. If it got much bigger, she would be engulfed in nothingness. In making the break from Dorf and The Daughters she had merely taken something out of her life without replacing the loss with something. Now she was terrified because there was nothing to stuff into the wound. The job. She tried to visualize herself as a teacher again. Things had changed in the past five years. Now there was little contact with those one taught. One stood bathed in hot light, spoke to a microphone and performed in front of a long-snouted black box.

"Today, children—" Would the pupils be children?

"Today, my dear pupils—" No, that was 1929 stuff, fifty years behind the time.

"Today we are taking up the subject of light in relation to shadow . . ." That was better, but exceedingly dull. Where was the color, the poetry and the passion of immortalizing life forms with oil and crayon? Where was the majesty and the meaning of art?

The expanding bag of nothingness inside her exploded in a dry sob, and Ella fought for control. Why were they in this drab little plane instead of a big four-hundred-passenger liner where one could cushion one's soul in the mingled ectoplasm emanating from many souls? Who were these strange creatures who had been chosen for this special flight? They were not the Beautiful People she had sought. They were drab, like the cabin of the little plane. She glanced around at the functional black plastic drapes over the tiny windows, the government-issue brown carpeting, grayish green seat covers stretched over skinny foam cushions. It was all so unpoetical, so crudely meaningless . . .

The words "Too late, too late," fluttered like obscene bats through the cavern of Alexander Curry's mind. The theme of lectures he had given for twenty-five years had embedded itself deeply in his subconscious. Only he had been honest enough with himself—as he had not been with audiences from whom he hoped to extract money—to admit that Too Late was really too late, without the chimera of "If-we-don't-wake-up-and-do-something."

The Great Stock Market Crash which took place on his twenty-first birthday had signaled the end of the World of Free Enterprise, he believed. It had wiped out his father's New York brokerage firm and had ended his own hopes of becoming a corporation lawyer. He'd had to leave Harvard and go to a grubby little college in Iowa where his mother's relatives lived. He worked his way through to a low-prestige sheepskin by pumping gas at a filling station. The Depression had wiped out two fortunes which would have descended to him, and as he watched them go, he felt that the hope of mankind had died with the 1929 crash. It had been Too Late for fifty years.

The hostess who by a careless blunder had extended his life beyond his means to remain independent, sauntered around the center clearing of the cabin glancing searchingly at each of the passengers. Curry looked up and their eyes met. He felt impelled to sharpen her attention on him.

"What time is it, please?"

A pixyish smile broke over the girl's face, and her eyes challenged him to an intellectual duel.

"It isth not yet too late, Misther Curree."

Embarrassed at having mumbled his thoughts aloud, he chose the sharpest of verbal swords which he had used on hecklers.

"Doomsday is Too Late."

She tossed her head airily. "We will decide that, Mister Curree, on the day after Doomsday."

Chapter IV

Group Two

—

Dr. Sylvester Markham, LL.D., with Ph.D.s in social science, education and the arts, chairman of the Social Science Department at the prestigious California University at Santa Cruz, presented a physique as imposing as his list of degrees and the titles of his published works. He was tall enough to carry his frontal bulge without appearing obese, and muscles, not fat, rippled on his heavy shoulders. From the varsity oars he had gone to water skiing, which he had continued into his fifties. Wind off salt water had toughened the skin under his luxuriant red-brown beard, but had faded the cobalt of his eyes to water-color blue. His manner was that of a benevolent despot, which he thought of himself as being; his voice was deeply mellifluous, but there were wary and crafty wrinkles around his smallish eyes. He crouched tense on the edge of a seat that was meant for reclining, not sitting.

As usual, he spoke without interruption. His audience, grouped around in a tight circle, was made up of six other social scientists, all of whom had been attending the annual convention of American Sociologists on the hilly campus of the University at Santa Cruz.

"From the private talk I had with the chap who—er—persuaded us to come along on this expedition, I gathered that we have been chosen as those most suitable to assist in molding a new, scientific society in the untamed regions of his country—presumably in Mongolia. There are all manner of nomads in that region beyond the Gobi, I understand, and they've been quite untouched by what we call civilization. We'll be starting from scratch, so to speak, to raise the level of their culture to the point where they can take their rightful place in the Family of Soviet Nations. In my studied opinion this is a most worthwhile project, and it serves to reflect the high ideals of the so-called enemy of our fascist government. We will now have a short question period."

No one spoke for a few throbbing seconds. The seven scientists, four men and three women, were seated in deeply cushioned, adjustable chairs arranged around a small cabin in a broken circle. The break in the circle was a companionway that led to lavatory, galley, and beyond to an operating compartment. None of the seven was quite sure how he had been conducted aboard the vessel, or craft, which was transporting them, supposedly, to a location in China. Most of these men and women, like much of the academic community, had been outspoken in support of the country which had squared off as Number One enemy of the United States. The days of childishly signing petitions and open-letter protests to the President and the Supreme Council of the United Nations had long since passed.

The sophisticated attitude of the time was one of frank friendship with the Enemy, to the point where animosities between the belligerents had been reduced to little more than a farce, albeit a one-sided farce. Spies spied—it was part of the game; a minor war, undeclared, of course, had been kept hotted up at some point on the globe in order to test new weapons, maintain production at its peak and eliminate surplus goods and population—the latter being the greatest concern of the Enemy. Proclamations were issued periodically by each side, but no one took them seriously. Until recently. Within the past few months the thunder of exhortations by leaders on both sides had taken on a more serious rumble, and there were indications that rifts within the long-splintered Red-bloc were healing. Thus, scales were tipping and the "kissing" had stopped.

There were provocations. For instance, insofar as anyone in the privy council knew, there had been no secret agreements or advance warning of "brain drain" kidnappings. It was most unsportsmanlike of the Enemy. Nuclear scientists, microbiologists, chemists, and others trained in techniques of modern warfare in the so-called White-bloc had been lured away or forcibly kidnapped from universities, research centers, and even from the most secret military installations. Oddly enough, these scientists did not, as demanded by protocol, come forth in the Enemy territory to denounce the Homeland and embrace the Enemy ideology. Both sides were becoming irritated over these incidents. The Red-bloc proclaimed its innocence; the White-bloc refused to believe. Both sides had long ago broken test-ban treaties and were busily saturating the atmosphere with dangerous radiation. A clash was imminent unless, in the words of the savants, "Something was Done."

Each of the seven scientists in this "brain drain" group fervently hoped and believed he had been selected because of his superior abilities and tolerant attitude to ease the tension between the two blocs. But they were collectively piqued because they were not given a free choice and because they had not been properly briefed.

Dr. Irma Boyd, thin, sere and slant-eyed, who headed the Department of Asian Studies at the Los Angeles University, was first to frame a question.

"Don't you agree, Doctor Markham, that the cultural uplift may be a long-range goal? There certainly doesn't appear to be any urgency about such a project as you describe. Do you not believe that our precipitous removal—"

"Abduction," someone supplied.

"—our abduction might not have been for the purpose of seeking a peaceful means to settle the present misunderstandings?"

Dr. Markham *harrumphed.* "Does not your question, Dr. Boyd, presuppose a situation in which peace is severely threatened?"

"Peace *is* severely threatened, and I say let's kill off the damned dove instanter! To hell with this harmony that's straining the patience of all of us! Let's do everything in our power to help the peace-loving bloc triumph over the rotten imperialism of the West! Then and then only can we have true peace, and only in peace can we build a stable society anywhere!"

The speaker was Dr. Vaughn Wright, youngest of the group and a one-time firebrand student demonstrator.

"Hear, hear!" chirped Dr. Eustice Emory-Leonard, a shriveled, bird-like gnome who wore glasses on a chain around his neck but never put them over his eyes. "Bloody dictators deserve to be smashed, so let's get about it!"

Albino-pale, pink-eyed Dr. Phillope Applebaum opened her pink-and-white mouth. All turned interested faces to the love-poet language instructor from Vassar. She dimpled enticingly as she spat, "Anyone with half a wit knows that the way to have peace is to *think* peace!"

"Where were we?" Dr. Markham panned around the circle with an indulgent paternal smile. "It appears that we're miles apart in our thinking—or should I say speculation? No doubt we will be properly briefed before we have to go into action of any sort."

"Might we not all be talking through our warbonnets?"

All eyes turned to the tall, loose-jointed man in his late sixties who had withdrawn from the others. Dr. Howard McMillan of Northwestern.

"Warbonnets, Dr. McMillan?" Dr. Markham questioned witheringly. "Don't you think your figure of speech is a bit strong for the academic inquiry in which we are engaged?"

McMillan lifted one eyebrow knowingly. "Stronger than your 'fascist' or Dr. Wright's 'rotten imperialism'?"

"But those are what one might call clichés of our intellectual circle, Dr. McMillan."

"Sorry to have violated the strict taboos of your tight little world, Dr. Markham. But if you will allow me, I wish to pose the question that we may be jumping to conclusions to take it for granted that our contact is from the Red-bloc. If my senses did not deceive me, I was treated to some kind of hypnotic hocus-pocus as that odd-looking man waved a bright rod in front of our faces. I don't remember boarding this craft, and I doubt if any of you do. We were talking in the hills one minute; the next we knew, a squat dark man who may have been mute appeared before us and brandished an eight- or nine-inch shiny rod. Then we were here. Let's face it—we may be the prisoners of a creature who isn't human."

"What utter nonsense!"

"Ridiculous!"

"Perfectly mad!"

"What fantastic imagination, Dr. McMillan!"

Everyone spoke at once. Dr. Markham indulged in a huge belly laugh, his paunch quaking like a disturbed pudding.

"Were you by any chance leading up to the conclusion, Dr. McMillan, that we may be aboard a flying saucer?"

The women shrieked, all but Dr. Laura Lighthouse Lindholm, whose rather plain face remained thoughtfully grave.

"Suppose we're streaking off at a speed greater than that of light toward the planet of a distant sun!" Dr. Emory-Leonard piped.

Dr. Lindholm's quiet countenance was rent by an explosion. "Of all the stupidly smug attitudes! Isn't it possible to communicate with you sawdust-filled academicians in language other than your own little clichés? Why not go on to say that the world is hollow and that we live in the center of it? Wasn't that the alleged belief of Adolf Hitler, Dr. Emory-Leonard? Didn't he hold to the theory that we were rattling around inside a hollow globe?"

The Oxford historian puffed out his insignificant chest. "Quite right. Shot anyone who disagreed with him."

The circle quieted, and hostility bristled on the faces of several.

"What is your point, Lindholm?" Dr. Markham pressed peevishly.

"Just this. There are a thousand million suns, or something like that, in our Community of Stars. It's reasonable to suppose that many of those suns have planets, and that many of the planets are habitable . . ."

"So a little green man from Mars comes along and kidnaps us in a flying saucer!" Vaughn Wright sneered.

Everyone but Dr. McMillan and Laura Lindholm laughed. They smiled knowingly at each other.

At that moment the lights went out and sleep descended on all of them like a curtain drawn.

Chapter V

When Dorf Allman slid under the wheel of the minicar at the jetport, she realized that she would have difficulty. She couldn't reach the foot pedals if she moved the seat back far enough to accommodate her belly behind the wheel. She tried to keep the big bubbly mass drawn in enough so she could steer the car, but unnatural breathing made her dizzy. She must, simply must, lose weight, she decided.

At the Wilson Avenue off-ramp she took a breath at the wrong moment. The car went out of control and smashed into a concrete wall. She lost weight. It dripped down on pedestrians and traffic below the ramp. An ambulance was called, but it never reached her.

In Chicago, as in other cities, police sirens shrieked madly as tired officers rushed from one scene of disaster to another. Violence had flared from spontaneous combustion when television and radio stations went off the air.

One police car raced north on Sheridan Road answering a call that had come from the parish house of St. Serafino's Church. The housekeeper was hysterical; there was something about having been lured away on a fake errand. When she got back she had found— She was unable to describe the horror she had found. The police did not reach their destination.

Two young housewives seated at a window that looked out on the sleeping Mauna Loa volcano discussed a problem that faced them. Ruth, the younger and more attractive of the sisters, drew deeply on her pink, cancer-tested cigarette.

"No matter how much Elsbeth likes her, Bart simply won't have her around. He can't stand her loud voice and all that coarse, 'home-made' stuff. I have a choice. I can have him or Mother. Which do you think it's going to be?"

Gerda, whose dark, rectangular face was totally unlike that of the grandmother for whom she had been named, took a sip of Instant and reached for one of her sister's cigarettes.

"Yuh. Billie and Teena adore her and ask me every day when 'grammother' will be here. But Doctor says I've got a heart condition; I'm not going to scrub every damned one of my floors on my hands and knees, like she insists on, or bake my own bread . . ."

"You forgot something." Ruth's lip curled away from the filter tip of her cigarette. "You have to raise the damned wheat and rye in organically fertilized fields, cut it with a hand scythe, and trample out the grain by hand . . ."

"By foot," Gerda laughed. "And where do we find a grist mill with a stone for grinding it?" Growing serious, she groaned, "Oh Lord, Lordie, I can't take any more of it! I get weak all over thinking about the arguments, the endless arguments. And besides, look what happened to Pop."

"He lost the argument," Ruth supplied bitterly.

"Yuh. We've got to do something."

They never did.

All passenger flights in and out of the O'Hare Jetport had been canceled. Persons waiting for them had been told several times that they must return home or go back to their temporary lodgings and wait for notification. Few had gone, not even at the personal urging of guards who circulated among them. Rumors flew and grew, taking on dark, ominous shapes that hovered over knots of chattering people. The groups began to move as if propelled by unseen giant hands; they came together to form a tornado of screaming, clawing, maddened humanity.

A soft-drink vending machine gave way first, spreading broken glass and rolling cans over the floor. The sound of rending metal and crunching plastic intoxicated the mob. Soon the cracking of bones and tearing of flesh added to the symphony of disaster. Children and old people and cripples were trampled, their bodies flattened like those of rabbits on a superhighway. The smell of blood and bursting guts awakened the jungle animal in the crowd. The shrieks and groans and howls that arose from the stampeding mob were hardly related to human sounds.

Plate-glass windows bowed outward from pressure, then cracked like cannon shot. Wild animals ran screaming out onto the deserted airfield to meet the waves of death that were merciful.

The October moon, plump and yellow in the empty sky, looked down upon a pocked surface like her own and thirstily drank the particles of oxygen and hydrogen that wafted her way. It had been a long, long time since she had had a drink.

Entry in the Diary

It happened, Mister Curry, much as you said it would, but it is fortunate for you that you were stonily unaware of the last-minute messages that were beamed to you. I am sorry that I intercepted them and lived vicariously through the horror in which your civilization exploded. But I am thereby made more hopeful of success next time. It is time now for music. Sleep, my passengers, sleep in the blind, unfeeling ignorance in which you have lived.

The lights dimmed in the little plane's cabin, and music that was at the same time haunting and soporific filled the small space. Like the voice which had summoned passengers from the Pan-United waiting room, it did not come through a conventional speaker, nor was it stereophonic. It came from all directions, dripping eerie notes into the dimly lit space. It was melodic, something from unknown woodwind instruments; at times it was like the cry of a human voice, sometimes the whistled notes of great birds and the love-calls of nonexistent animals. Half-notes, sub-notes, tortured high notes glided into full-bodied theme, then faded to echoes from distant icy slopes. It was mountain music, but it spoke, too, of great distances and cold space.

It was nothing from the Alpine region, Alexander Curry decided. Himalayan, perhaps. Ella thought it was something from the High Andes, where rarefied air was too thin to support a stream of sound. Whatever the origin or the manner of conveying it to the cabin, it had a soothing effect.

One by one the passengers dropped their gnawing anxieties and floated in tranquillity. Osta concluded that the rat poison in the blueberry muffins that had killed Wilbur Eisen had gotten there as the result of an unavoidable error. Roy Hamilton, teetering on the edge of his drunken stupor, was sure that the sweet little black-market deal he had lined up in the Islands would bring him the fabulous wealth he craved, and Ella mentally made peace with the snouted black instrument she must teach. The man in priest's garb dropped the little book he did not understand and leaned back, exposing his crooked, once-broken nose. Brock and Nadine renewed their temporary faith in each other, and Pretty Bean reached the conclusion that three illegitimate babies were enough for the time being. Joe Quail didn't care one way or another. He didn't suffer from white people's anxieties and hungers. Brother Smith browsed with his beloved goats on a heavenly green hillside, and Hugh Shipsted was happy to be reunited with Tana. Vera Simpson remembered the china-painting she had done as a girl—dainty flowers and sprays set off with gold and silver scrolls. She must take it up again when opportunity permitted.

Alexander Curry alone remained awake and thoughtful.

Craft II

Dr. Howard McMillan and Laura Lindholm did not sleep as soundly as did the others. They were aware of a steward, who might have been the contact man, tiptoeing among them, drawing stiff drapes across the portholes, closing vents and fastening acceleration harness on the sleepers. In a short time, the seven within the black-dark little cabin were trussed like cocoons in foam-cushioned reclining seats.

Before long—or it may have been eons during which they were miraculously preserved—a blue light seeped into the cabin around the tightly drawn porthole covers. It was so intensely blue that it dominated all other waves of radiation. It was sight and sound and cosmic vibration. Howling banshees of sound tore at the craft and threatened to devour or dissolve it; shafts of light lanced at it and at the writhing bodies of the sleepers within the cabin. Huge waves of unassembled matter tossed the tiny ship; monsters of the strange deep growled, and gigantic tusks tore at it.

When at last the punishing blue began to fade into the green spectrum and the high decibels of sound diminished somewhat, Dr. McMillan cautiously and painfully opened his eyes. Dr. Lindholm did likewise, and their puzzled glances met. He winked; she smiled and held out a trembling hand. He took it. Then they slept soundly and peacefully.

Chapter VI

Group One

Alexander Curry was not sure how or when they had all been neatly laced, like papooses, onto their reclining chairs. Everyone but him was soundly asleep, even the infant bound to the side of Pretty Bean. The stewardess had somehow managed to fasten herself into the seat nearest the companionway. Curry guessed that they had long ago escaped the gravity of earth—that must have taken place before the first awakening, although he had noticed no signs of weightlessness.

When the flash came, he thought he was dreaming it.

A vivid blue light sliced through the cabin with searing incandescence. The music ceased abruptly, and the passengers stirred. There were a few gasps and frightened groans, and Vera Simpson emitted a high, thin shriek of animal terror, which subsided to a series of barks and finally to panting sobs. Nadine whimpered, the priest thrashed about, straining at his bindings, and Ella wept audibly. All, even the stewardess, were affected physically.

Curry found he was twisting, groaning, and crying out. Goblins howled, the little craft quivered and creaked; burning blue that was light and sound and vibration assaulted it from every side. It spun around, tossed and dropped into cavernous depths that all but tore it apart. But it held together, and all passengers survived the ordeal. They rode out the storm of blue, and when a friendly greenish light began to seep through the tightly drawn curtains over the portholes, the stewardess unstrapped herself and moved among the passengers examining them tenderly and unfastening the webbing straps that bound them. The engineer, wearing a black headpiece pushed back from his eyes, came to the companionway and waited until she had finished. The smaller infant of Pretty Bean was cyanotic; the stewardess shook it gently, then breathed into its mouth until it cried. Bennett signaled with his wand-rod, and she responded by holding up hers. He returned forward.

The passengers stirred, the lights came up, and music resumed, long, galloping waves of the strange rhythm. It might have been wind forcing its way through fissures in rock. It rose from a limestone whistle to a quartz shriek, but the counterpoint was from seasoned wood, resonant, restrained. It told a melodic story of suffering and bravery, of despair that sought and found hope. It was curiously tranquillizing.

The cubist lines on Vera Simpson's face relaxed, the priest retrieved the prayerbook, caressed it, then slipped it into a pocket. Osta Eisen hugged her granddaughter to her, but remained immersed in her *weltschmerz*. Nadine repaired her makeup while Brock regarded her quizzically. Ella Pozniak dry-washed her face and surreptitiously crossed herself.

Hamilton yawned and lurched out of his seat heading toward the lavatory. When he emerged from it he turned toward the operators' compartment. The stewardess blocked his way.

He pushed her aside, but still could not pass her: "Don't interfere with the men's work, Baby. I'm going up front and show these gooks how to fly this crate. It's been bobbing all around."

The girl smiled sweetly. "You will return to your seat, Mister Hamilton. On this flight you are a passenger."

"That's what *you* think. Out o' my way, now, before I have to get rough."

She fenced with her wand. He reeled and grappled with her. Then Bennett stepped out of the forward compartment, laid his stick against Hamilton's neck, and led the subdued pilot back to his seat.

Hamilton slumped and began to hum "Sweet Bay-bee Gurrl with a corkscrew currl . . ."

The craft settled to the ground like a bird alighting, bounced and bumped rapidly for a mile or more, then tottered like a drunken crane over an unsmoothed surface for another mile and came to a fluttering stop.

The passengers stretched up to the portholes and pawed aside the curtains. There were no buildings or other craft in sight. The plane rested on the cracked, uneven surface of a rock-strewn alkali desert, the gray-white ground flecked here and there with streaks of terra-cotta and also with white markings, evidently parts of a huge design.

Hamilton popped upright in his seat. "Crissake, what have these gooks done?"

"We have just landed our aircraft, Mister Hamilton." The flight captain, holding his swagger stick-wand like a weapon, stepped through the companionway.

Hamilton leaped out of his seat and faced him. "Don't you know better'n to land this rickety old box o' bolts on rough ground? You got it in for insurance companies, or something?"

"It was done, Hamilton. There is nothing to discuss. Men out first, please."

"Just a little minute!"

Hamilton tried to push past the captain to the flight deck. "This is not the Hall Jetport of Honolulu or any Goddamn' place. If this crate's in running order, I'm going to take it and get us somewhere."

The engineer barred his way. "All your 'Somewheres' are 'Nowheres' now, Hamilton. We have come down on the only usable landing field on the face of this earth. Shall we get out?"

Hamilton did not yield. "Not a damn thing doing! If what you say is true, there's one hell of a war going on, and I've got some mighty important things to do. Anybody with me?"

Joe Quail stepped forward.

Feeling that he was supported, Hamilton lunged and drove a fist at the engineer's jaw.

The blow did not land. With a lightning-like swipe the captain deflected it with his stick. Hamilton reeled groggily, although he had been barely touched.

Joe Quail dropped into Nadine's lap. No one spoke. The flight captain sheathed his weapon in his sleeve and nodded to the engineer who opened the door, swinging it downward like a ramp. It was steep, but cleated. The captain and the engineer descended first.

Curry followed, taking the captain's proffered hand. Hugh Shipsted came after him, then Robert Smith and the priest, who got his feet tangled in the long cloak he had hastily donned. Hamilton and Quail remained inside whispering; the engineer busied himself pulling baggage from an opening underneath the plane. When he emerged laden with bags, Quail leaped on him, pinning him to the ground. Hamilton then threw himself on the captain, scissoring his legs around the tall man's neck. Smith and Shipsted stood apart, stunned by the sudden action, and Brock Gunnison remained in the doorway.

The priest hurried to the scattered luggage, pulled out a black case, opened it, and scrabbled in it frantically.

Inside the cabin the women huddled together. Pretty Bean sobbed, her infants wailed, and Elsbeth clung whimpering to her grandmother. Osta scolded and tried to push past Brock, but he held her back.

The man in priest's cloth found words as he reached something in the suitcase.

"Hamilton take plane. We go to City. You listen to me. I speak AUTHORITY!" He roared the last word as he started to withdraw his hand from the tumble of clerical garments.

Bennett, who had bested Quail, flung himself at the black-garbed man, immobilizing the hand in the suitcase with a charge from his metal rod. He then grappled with the cleric.

Brock Gunnison leaped clumsily from the doorway and pulled the engineer off the back of the black-garbed man.

"Haven't you any respect for priesthood? He's a holy man . . ."

Bennett wielded his metal rod to best advantage, stunning both Brock and the priest. As he was about to rise, he was felled again, this time by Brother Smith, who goat-butted him. Smith tumbled into the melee, arms and legs waving.

Hugh Shipsted looked on, bewildered, not sure which were the Goodies whom he should help and which were Baddies whom he should attack.

Curry, who had made a life-long practice of staying aloof from the quarrels of others, walked off into the strange desert. There was a thin rawness to the air, he noticed, nothing like the snow-laden cold which was descending on Chicago when they departed. This air was parched, as was the ground underfoot, and there was a peculiar red murkiness in the sky. He was sure the plane had landed on a high plateau—but where? There was a broken ring of high mountains around the area, unfinished-looking mountains without vegetation or the softening effects of erosion, and from some of the sawtooth peaks rose smoke and spits of flame. He then realized that the air was thick with volcanic cinders, which fell like light, warm rain and drifted into terra-cotta-colored ridges on the alkali ground. Although he had covered most of the civilized world, this was not a location he recognized. The altitude was too high for a Pacific island, and he knew of no region where volcanoes were so prevalent. Had a series of nuclear explosions suddenly activated them? He discarded that theory when he noticed that the cinders underfoot showed a fall of months, perhaps years.

Fright of the Unknown began to clutch at his throat when the sharp cries and grunts of combatants near the plane demanded his attention. He hurried back.

"Stop this at once!" he commanded. "Nothing is to be gained by senseless fighting. We need all our combined mental faculties. We're in a strange location . . ."

"Oh, no, we're not." Brother Smith extricated himself from the jumble of bodies on the ground. "I know this place—been here too many times. It's the Bonneville Salt Flats."

Curry did not voice his doubt.

The women crowded up to the door straining to listen, but were held back by the stewardess, who stood poised as if for flight. The engineer and captain started toward Smith, but she signaled them with her rod, indicating they should allow him to continue. The women spilled down the steps, the stewardess assisting them. They remained in a huddled group with eyes on Smith.

Feeling himself the center of attention, he puffed up proudly.

"See them dirt-dump hills over there—" He indicated some foothills that bore the same raw, unfinished look of the mountains. "My ranch is a little to the south on yonder side of them, about fifteen, twenty miles from here. It's quite a hike, but you're all welcome to stay there till they get the plane fixed so's we can go on to Honolulu. The Indians I left there to look after my goats can put us up somehow, and there's plenty of grub, such as it is."

Hamilton pawed at the captain. "Why didn't you tell us you had engine trouble—that is, if you've got an engine in that screwy thing. I never heard a whisper from it. I'll just take a look at it." He started toward the plane.

"Come back!" the captain commanded sharply.

Hamilton started to run, but stumbled. The captain pounced on him, plied his metal rod, and dragged him back to the circle, glassy-eyed as he had been when he was drunk.

The passengers were restive. Several spoke at once.

"Why did we land?"

"What happened?"

"Are we going to turn back?"

"Is there anything to eat?" This from Joe Quail, who was again helping Pretty Bean with her two wailing infants.

The crew consulted with each other silently, but none of them offered any suggestions. They were obviously waiting for the passengers to take the initiative.

Osta Eisen delved into her voluminous lunch kit and brought forth sandwiches and jars of food which she instructed Elsbeth to pass to Pretty Bean and the other women. The little girl offered the last sandwich to the stewardess, who suddenly remembered her responsibility.

"There is some food in our—how you say?—kitchen. I will get." She disappeared into the plane.

Brother Smith stood, still at the center of the group, awaiting response to his invitation. Curry, never at a loss for words to fit any occasion, stepped into the breach.

"Apparently the crew is reluctant to inform you of something that was made clear to me, perhaps only to me, since I did not sleep as soundly as the rest of you . . ."

"*Ja, ja,* we know," Osta interrupted. "It has come already the atom bombs—big flashes in the sky. Maybe we're all that's left in the world, yet, and all we got is what we brought with us. I think we take up Brother Smith's good invitation and get there before more poison chemicals fall on us from the sky."

"You took the words right out of my mouth," Smith said, sweeping a hand around the horizon. "The wrath of the Lord has rained down on all them wicked cities, and He arranged it so's those He decided to save would have a haven. All I ask is that those of you who accept my hospitality act in accordance with Christian decency." He fixed his attention on the crimson-clad Nadine.

"Amen!" Vera Simpson barked, glaring first at Pretty Bean and Joe Quail, then at Brock and Nadine.

"This is hardly a time to be too strictly selective," Curry put in hastily. "By the grace of the good Lord—and our rescuers—we have been saved from incineration. It is also our great good fortune to have the offer of a refuge. I suggest we set out at once in order to get as far as possible in the daylight. From the position of the sun I judge it to be about three o'clock."

"Three-forty, Central Time." Hugh Shipsted found his voice.

All eyes turned questioningly to him, and he felt obligated to explain his watch. He held up the wrist on which it was strapped.

"It was my grandfather's—the ticking kind, so they let me keep it."

"Keep it wound so we'll have some way of knowing the time," Brock Gunnison admonished.

"For what?" asked Nadine from the depths of hopelessness. With sagging shoulders and listless movements she turned toward the pile of luggage. "Someone will have to help me carry my bags."

Bennett, the engineer, came forward to take them from her hand. "You won't have to carry them. We have something . . ." He moved to the trapdoor under the plane and pulled out a hand sled with runners curled back at the front and decorated in the same sort of Aztec manner as the receptacle used for watches at the jetport. He began loading bags and suitcases on it.

"*They* are not going with us!" Vera Simpson screeched, pointing at the engineer.

"Are they not our rescuers, Miss Simpson?" Curry soothed.

With a throaty growl, the spinster subsided.

The stewardess appeared in the doorway holding two trays. She looked with dismay at the crowd that was trailing after Brother Smith into the desert.

"Let me help you, Tana."

Hugh Shipsted sprang up the steep ramp to take one of the trays. He then stood holding it, undecided. The other passengers were moving away while the crew remained to consult silently with each other, rods twinkling. At length the stewardess noticed the dilemma of the man who adored her.

"You may go later with us, if you wish, Hugh Shipsted. We must collect some things from the plane which we will take on another sled."

"I wouldn't go without you, Tana."

She smiled tenderly at the man who was so like a child. "Eat the food, Hugh. It will be a long walk." She seated herself and pulled him down beside her, and they ate while the engineer and captain busied themselves around the craft.

Chapter VII

"Not much farther, folks. See that little round hill over there?"

Smith, who led the procession of weary, staggering walkers, pointed to a knoll of volcanic ask, pink in the slanting sunrays. "I recognize it right enough, 'cause it's on my property. Buildings are just the other side of it."

It was doubtful if anyone heard him. Hearing was dulled with fatigue, and each of the travelers was wrapped in his own sorrow and worry. Osta, carrying her seven-year-old granddaughter like a sack of meal with a strangling grip around the girl's middle, bounded past Brother Smith.

"If we walk like we had some life in us it wouldn't seem so far." She didn't walk, however; she ran. Joe Quail, running, caught up with her. He carried the wailing and wet Bakie Bean on his shoulders piggy-back.

"Better not get ahead of Brother Smith, or you'll get lost," he cautioned. "This is tricky country, full of mirages and queer shadows. You aren't always where you think you are."

Osta slowed and set Elsbeth on her feet.

"Not me get lost," she argued. "I've got a compass built into my head. He points sout' and I go sout' till I come to his ranch."

"I've got a compass built in my head, too," Joe Quail said, "and mine says we're going north by east."

"Then the sun is out of order," Osta countered, pointing to a blaze that flared on the horizon. "Since when does the sun go to bed in the east?"

"Since when," Joe Quail asked soberly, "does the sun come up in the west? We walked all night."

"And I suppose I walked in my sleep?"

"You did, *Grossmutter*, you did!" Elsbeth piped. "It was night a long time, and I was asleep sometimes while you carried me."

The older woman whirled on Quail as though it were his fault that she was confused. "You look like one of Them. Can you talk with metal rods?"

Quail shrugged, almost dislodging the precariously perched boy. "No, but I bet I could learn."

The little girl tugged at her grandmother's pantaloons. "We'll be late to see *Grossmutterchen* if we don't hurry."

Osta frowned at her warningly. Others had come alongside and were looking with mild curiosity at the woman and the Indian.

"Will Great-grandmother be waiting for us?" Elsbeth pressed.

Osta shushed her. "We won't talk about that now, dear."

The stewardess paused beside the German woman and the little girl. Quail moved on.

Osta bridled defensively. "I do not give away the little game. I told her after while we see the *Grossmutterchen.*"

The stewardess, whom by now everyone called Tana, bent and cupped the child's chin in her hand.

"It will be a long time before you see your grandmamma's mother. You must be patient."

"Will we be in Heaven then?"

"Oh, no." The stewardess smiled down on the little girl. "You don't go to your Heaven until after you are dead. You are very much alive, are you not?"

"Yes, I'm alive."

"That's good to know," Pretty Bean put in plaintively. "I'd begun to wonder, myself."

Nadine's shoes were little more than shreds, and she leaned heavily on a dispirited Brock. Her makeup was raddled and her hair awry, but she still wore her velvet gloves and clutched the velvet purse.

"Did you ever see a crustier bunch to get stuck with at the end of the world?"

Brock grunted something unintelligible.

"Funny," Nadine went on, loosing the thoughts that had been festering within her mind. "Always I imagined Henry and I would be together when the end came. We talked about it a lot. There'd be a bright flash somewhere below where the old Empire State Building stood, and we'd run down the apartment house stairs, then down the steps to the East River. We'd hold hands and wade out into the dirty water and drown together before the next bomb hit. Then we'd float away, each of us wearing halos of garbage, and little fish bumping into us."

"Don't see how there could be any fish left alive in the East River," Brock mumbled sourly.

"Well, it can't come true now, anyway."

"Maybe you'll get your wish yet. This is probably just a bad scare, like all the others. Probably there'll be some rescue planes out looking for us before long."

Vera Simpson marched up alongside Brother Smith. "Do you think this visitation of the wrath of God will herald the Second Coming?"

"Huh?" The missionary pulled himself out of a reverie. "Just hope my goats are all right. You think goats don't have feelings, but they're really very sensitive. Sorry I had to leave them with the Indians, but I had no choice. The Lord's work comes first."

"How right you are, Brother Smith."

They had entered a narrow valley and Smith paused to guide his guests. He waved his hand to indicate the view across a narrow thread of water that trickled around gray boulders and patches of shrubbery.

"See them chalk cliffs there. That's the location of the caves where I stored canned goods and ammunition. Good thing I read all them old Civil Defense manuals, ain't it? We can eat for a long time."

"Ach!" Osta barked scornfully. "Chalk, you say! You must have smoked an awfully big pipe to get them that black!"

"The cliffs look black because they're in a shadow, Mistress Eisen," Tana put in quickly, toying with her wand.

Curry, who agreed with Osta Eisen, realized that it was expedient to see what the stewardess wanted them to see.

"Of course it's the shadows!" he said with more enthusiasm than he felt. "We're all so tired we can't see straight. I suggest we leave the discussion of our surroundings until we have rested."

"Well said, Mister Curry," the missionary agreed.

They passed through an opening in a crumbling stone wall and followed a path through dense shrubbery to come out shortly on a clearing dotted with small buildings.

"Here we are at my ranch," Smith said expansively. "I want all of you to feel right at home. Like the old Spanish grandees used to say, *'Mi casa su casa.'* That means my house is your house."

He broke off to stare in jaw-dropping astonishment as the weary group staggered to benches which were ranged around the clearing. Crew members conferred in a tight huddle, rods twinkling.

Smith was shaken, but he babbled on to no one in particular.

"Can't figure this out. A lot o' changes has been made. Looks like Bolly—that's the Indian I left to take care of my goats and the place—has made himself mighty busy. I got to find him."

Instead of the sprawling frame ranch house he had left, there was a group of eight or ten trim fieldstone cottages ranged around a smoothly swept courtyard. A huge outdoor oven stood to one side, and there was a long table in front of it and a shed beside it. Long-handled cooper cooking utensils of various shapes hung in the shed, where there was a worktable and some pottery that was decorated in the Aztec-like designs.

In near-mad bewilderment Smith mumbled to himself. "Mom's kitchen garden was here, and the porch was there, where she sat in her rocker singing the old-time hymns. I can hear her now . . ." With something like a sob he sank to his knees and turned a tear-wet face upward.

"Rock of ages, cleft for me; Let me hide myslf in Thee . . ."

A tall man dressed in Indian-blanket robes and laced sandals stood over him and spoke soothingly.

"I'm sorry I couldn't let you know about the changes, Misser Smith, but I did not know where to reach you."

"Bolly!"

Smith scrambled to his feet and looked up at the dark, rectangular face.

"You've changed! Everything's changed! What happened?"

"After the old house burned down, it seemed like a good idea to build these small stone cabins. Some of my wife's people came to live with us, but there is plenty of room for all."

Smith sniffled and mopped his face. "Gave me 'n awful funny feeling, getting home to a place that wasn't home. How are my goats? You take good care of them?"

"The best, Misser Smith. You'll find that they have changed, too." He led the way up an incline to a thicket of thorny shrubs and through a gate to a stone-walled enclosure. There, twelve or fifteen dun-colored animals browsed on tender shoots of the shrubs.

Smith whistled and called, "Nancy! Where are you, Nancy?"

The Indian laid a sympathetic hand on the missionary's arm. "I'm afraid, Misser Smith, she is not here."

"Not here! But I thought you said my goats were all right."

"It is things that happen which we must endure, my brother," the Indian intoned sadly. "You see, there were twin kids, and they were very large . . ." Before the slow-thinking Smith had reacted, he added brightly, "The young ones are gentle and affectionate, and the female is much like Nancy. You will love them very much."

He pushed a young animal forward, and Smith fell to his knees to clasp it around the neck.

"She is very sweet. Just like my Nancy. What's her name?"

"It is your privilege to name her, Misser Smith, and her twin brother also." He indicated the twin, which had come up to nuzzle his hand.

Smith embraced it also. "My lovelies, my beautiful little friends. You both look like your sweet mother. I'll call you—" He caressed first one, then the other. "I'll call you Mabel and Abel. Can't give you both Biblical names and have them rhyme. Can you think of any, Bolly?"

Before the Indian could reply, there was a commotion in the brush and Osta Eisen pushed through.

"Breakfast is all ready on the table, Brother Smith. You were so busy schmooching with the *gurs* you didn't hear us call, I guess."

"The girls? Ha, that's a good one. Cold day in summer when I'd be schmooching with the girls." He rose and dusted off his knees, waiting for a response to his intended humor.

Osta and the tall man were staring fixedly at each other, their eyes locked in communication.

She spoke in a small, impatient voice to Smith. "The goats, I meant. Go get now your breakfast before it gets cold."

Smith left, but Osta and the tall man remained in silent communication. The gaze broke at length, and she appraised his high, square forehead, like her own, the almond-shaped eyes, the rough-hewn shoulders and the strong, long-fingered hands.

"So," she accused aloud, "I come at last to mein own *Vater!* I wait almost fifty years for the father who should have been with *Mutter* und me when I was born!"

He leaned down to imprison the woman's hands in his own. "My dear child," he intoned, "much as I should like to have been with you and your wonderful mother at that time, I could not . . ." He ceased oral speech and again locked gaze with hers, this time plying the bright rod he withdrew from a sleeve.

With a gasp that was almost a cry of pain Osta broke the connection.

"*Nein!* It is not possible! You make fun of me, you stuff me with terrible lies!" She turned and ran through the thicket, paying no heed to the thorns that tore her clothing and skin.

The man caught up with her and pinioned her flailing arms with his. "It is a truth you must live with, Osta-Na. When you have calmed yourself, after you have eaten and rested, I will take you to your mother. She must not see you in this agitated state. She is ageing and frail, much older at seventy than I am at one hundred and twenty."

Osta quieted, but remained in her father's arms. "I must make a nest in my mind for these strange things, *Vater.*" She reflected a moment, then asked, "The young man who came to me at the O'Hare Jetport with the question about *Mutter,* is he my brother?"

He released her and they made their way along the path toward the courtyard. "Gar-Na is your half brother, the son of my fourth wife. But he loves our Gerda as much as he does his own mother."

"The other man, is he, too, my brother? And the girl?"

"No, Ben-Ad is only a friend and a very capable navigator. He was my engineer when I flew a *dzo*. The young woman, Id-Mar-Ok, is a volunteer worker at our Project here. She is one of Precious Blood. That cannot be explained in either of your languages, but it means that she is a descendant of The People—the ones who came here from somewhere else and started our ancestors climbing the ladder toward what we are pleased to call civilization."

"Whew!" Osta brushed at her head with her hands. "Like bees those strange thoughts fly around! Maybe I don't want them to sting me!"

"You cannot brush them away, dear child."

"Tell me this, *Vater*. If things had been, I mean, well— If they had been natural, what would have been my name?"

The man laughed with full-bodied mirth. "My dear daughter, to introduce myself, I am Shur-Et-Na. You are Osta-Na."

"Osta-Na . . . Osta-Na . . . Osta-Na . . . It is good after so long a time to have a name, even if it does sound like something made up in a fictitious story."

Chapter VIII

Group Two

Dr. Markham lifted one foot and looked with dismay at the abraded sole of his walking sandal.

"Beastly stuff, this Gobi sand. Unless the Chin-coms can supply us with some wooden shoes or something that can withstand this broken glass sand, we'll be in a big fat fix before long."

"Maybe the Russians seeded the area with a lot of ground-up vodka bottles," Dr. Emory-Leonard added with a wheezing giggle. His own English-made shoes were faring worse than Dr. Markham's sandals.

"What do you think I've been walking on for the past six or ten miles?" Phillope Applebaum's baby-pink skin was scorched beet red, face, shoulders and legs. She had used her short wrap-around skirt as a sun-shield first for the face, then the shoulders, and now she was wearing it as a skirt was intended to be worn, but it reached only a few inches below her buttocks. Her acrylic plastic shoes were as near to glass slippers as anything in the way of footwear, but they had not withstood the sharp particles in the soil. She held up one of the shoes.

"I can assure you, the grit I'm walking on is my own."

Irma Boyd limped forward in the straggling line. "I hope they don't set the imperialistic blooodhounds on us. I'm leaving blood prints."

"Try again, won't you, Irma, to see if you can't communicate with our worthy guide or guru, or whatever you call him." This from Dr. Vaughn Wright, whose enthusiasm for the mission had wilted along with his glossified Dacron shirt.

"Might as well talk to a wooden Indian in a museum," she snapped. "This man doesn't know any of the dialects with which I am familiar—I've tried them all. If you ask me, I think he's just a lackey, an errand boy sent out to collect us. He's no more perceptive or mentally alert than those cretin peasants who are pulling our luggage sled. Or maybe they're all dumb mutes; they never seem to talk except with those shiny sticks."

Dr. McMillan, who had the good fortune to be wearing stout walking shoes, had maintained his objectivity along with the skin on his feet.

"I've observed our—er, ah—escorts quite closely, and I'm sure they communicate on a mind-to-mind basis and use the sticks as mere aids—for emphasis, or something of that sort."

"Have you intercepted any of their mental messages, Dr. McMillan, that would give us a clue as to where we're going and how far we are from the destination?" Markham asked with open sarcasm.

McMillan ignored the thrust. "I still think we'd have been better off to have traveled at night instead of shivering under those thorny bushes and now blistering under the sun that would have at least warmed us while we were resting."

"If we have to cross the entire Gobi Desert, as it appears we're going to do, we'll have plenty of opportunity to try out different plans of travel," Irma Boyd put in witheringly.

Laura Lindholm, whose stork-like gait had saved the soles of her shoes, loped up at this point.

"We're no more in the Gobi Desert than we are on the moon! There are no volcanoes like these in China or any part of Asia. And surely you can all see that you're walking in cinders, not on sand."

"Volcanoes! Cinders!" Wright scoffed. "Mirages. Next you'll tell us there's a big lake up ahead, with swans on it and weeping willows dipping their branches into it. If your disordered mind is playing tricks on you, Dr. Lindholm, I suggest you keep your delusions to yourself."

"Now, now," Dr. Markham scolded. "Let's refrain from acrimony. Our tempers are frayed like our shoes, and the heat is liquefying our brains, but we must retain our objectivity . . ."

Phillope Applebaum whipped off her skirt with a snap and threw it over her head as a babushka.

"Objectivity, my—" She waggled thinly covered buttocks. "And heat of the sun! You're all daft, perfectly mad! I'm freezing!" Her teeth chattered.

Dr. Emory-Leonard drew his jacket around his thin shoulders. "It is a bit on the chilly side, but maybe I haven't thawed out yet. There was ice—"

Laura Lindholm whooped. "Look up ahead! Some cliffs, trees . . . and it looks like water!"

Dr. Wright laughed loudly. "What did I say about a mirage?"

At that moment the guide turned and gesticulated with his metal rod. He grinned, nodded, and caught the attention of everyone, then pointed to the oasis that loomed solidly ahead.

"He says, 'Not much farther, folks,' " Irma Boyd translated, then added somewhat sourly, "We'll get a little rest, at least."

Dr. Wright groaned. "I hope not another trek tomorrow! What I can't understand is why that plane had to land so damned far from the oasis. Not when there was the whole desert to land in."

"We came down at some sort of landing field," Laura Lindholm pointed out. "Didn't you notice the runways outlined in white stones and the direction signs and other markings?"

"Seeing things again, Dr. Lindholm?" Wright sneered.

"Shouldn't we conserve our energy for the last hundred-yard dash?" Dr. McMillan put in.

He was answered with hostile glares from those around him. For years he had been the recipient of hostility, and he had developed defenses, but in this small group under the unusual circumstances it was difficult to refrain from communicating. He moved to Laura Lindholm's side.

She reached out a hand and he took it. The warmth of offered friendship poured over him, and he felt some of his barriers weakening.

"What do you think, Laura?" He wanted to make a longer speech, but he found that his lip was trembling.

She flashed a womanly smile at him. "I think we shouldn't feed the animals. They're about to go berserk."

Chapter IX

The Diary

No sooner had I seated myself in the conveyance for the departure port than I realized my inner core had been touched. I had had to use my kay *to its limit to conceal my entrance at the place they called Rockford. Foolishly, I had exhausted my supply of the currency which Gar-Na had given me before I went out exploring. The man in the seat near the one I took became aware of my presence almost at once. At first I was annoyed with myself because I had not seated myself beside one of the unimaginative lumps who could not break out of the image pattern I had implanted. I had made the mistake of assuming that all the people of that time and place were lumps.*

Also, I made the mistake of trying to look like one of Them by applying gum to my lips. How did those uncouth, semi-savage women manage to so expertly alter their faces? I was clumsy, pitiably so, and the man beside me reached out a pseudopod of sympathy! I tasted the sweet of pure tenderness which intensified as he became involved in a self-deception. His was a child's dependent love for its mother, a wistful groping for life understanding mingled with an adolescent proclamation of protectiveness.

Most embarrassing was the fact that he had mistaken me for the woman with whom he was going to seal a matehood. That was due to my own blunder in trying to probe him. He is much more sensitive than I had suspected, and he had felt the ging-wing *caress of the current I sent through his emotional center. Instead of the suspicion and indignation with which most persons respond to probes, he reacted with an emanation of love. Then his upper-mind rationalized, and he convinced himself that I was the object of his love. One he called Tana was that object, therefore I was Tana!*

Having been touched by his childish tenderness, I was unwilling to perform the operation necessary to destroy the love-image in his mind. Even when he called me by the despised name of Tana, I was flattered and moved by his attention. He had aroused in me that quality so near the surface of my emotional being, the protective love of a female for its young. I wanted to caress and cuddle this man of the twentieth century as I would a little helpless gur. *Now I find myself maternally attached to the poor creature, who is floundering in a world he does not understand. Or is this the quality of love? Never before have I been stirred in this manner, and I am reluctant to give a name to my strange emotion.*

Gar-Na was amused by my predicament, and of course he communicated his version of it to his father. Shur-Et-Na is saddened and disappointed in me, I think. He has not been able to screen completely his hope that I would become one of Gar-Na's wives. Our Project Leader, despite his high gloss of culture, retains a primitive reverence for the Precious Blood. It would please him greatly to have his family strains mingled with those of the Clan of Ok-Nokken.

I must tread softly. I do not want to provoke the displeasure of the Leader and thereby create unpleasantness at work, and I do not want to leave the Project. More precisely, I do not want to be separated from Hugh.

Shame come to me, and sorrow on my parents, but I, Id-Mar-Ok of the Precious Blood from our Mother World, degenerately wish to live as the "Tana" girl of a non-communicant semi-savage of the twentieth century! May the Flame of Oom find me in my darkness!

Chapter X

"You got any ideas about this fruity shanghai we got caught in?"

Hamilton threw the question at the dozing Joe Quail after they had been politely ushered to one of the cottages, then locked in. Their beds were straw-stuffed pallets on the floor, but if the sleeping accommodations were crude, the illumination was more sophisticated than any known to them. Dim light came for no discernible outlet, but from everywhere, as had the music in the plane cabin.

The brightly colored blankets that covered the pallets were woven of a very soft wool in geometric patterns, not unlike those made on hand looms by the Indians of Western United States and Mexico. There was a high-altitude chill in the air, and the men had covered themselves.

The Indian put a hand over his exposed ear. "Turn down the volume, flyboy. I'm not in the next county."

Hamilton kicked off his blanket and bounced to his feet. "Let's get something straight right now, Tamale. I'm the only one of this fornicatin' bunch that's got the brains and the guts to get us out of here. We're some kind of prisoners of war—that was made mighty clear during that little squabble at the plane. But I'm not buying the brainwashing the others have fallen for. Not me, Laosy Hamilton, not after all the training I had in Asia. They're mighty cute, these Manchurian voodoo men or whatever they are, flashing little bright rods around to do a hypnotism act. But I got eyes—I noticed you didn't buy the whole store. Only you've fallen for that big-bellied chick . . ."

Quail sat up. "You're out of line, Laosy. You get this straight—"

Hamilton retreated, fending off an attack with outstretched hands. "All right, all right. We'll leave the chirp out of it. All I'm asking you to do is to get into line with me and help with the others. Or all of us snakes will find ourselves in the middle of this Red desert without a spot to hiss in."

Quail lay down. "Very funny, Hamilton. State your case. I'm not afraid of anything I've seen so far."

The flyer flexed his muscles in shadow-boxing. "You implying that I'm scared o' these gooks? Just because I kept my yap shut and tailed along to this goat ranch doesn't mean I'm buying their fairy tales."

"Ranch!" Quail exclaimed. "You bought some of their bag o' bones if you think we're on a ranch."

"All right, all right, call it what you want to. But I sure as hell know Utah when I see it—flown over it too many times."

"I see. Just what do you propose to do?"

"I should tell you in this screwy little box! Don't you think I know they got the place bugged?"

"Umph!" Quail flipped over, turning his back on Hamilton and settling himself for sleep. He never ceased to wonder at the unfathomable stupidity and unbounded vanity of white people. At least the captors, whoever they were, were not cursed with white skins. It might be interesting to see what they had to offer. As he dropped into his usually dreamless sleep, Joe Quail decided that he was glad he had been among those saved.

Long after the others had been taken to cabins for the night, the man in priest's clothing sat on a bench to one side of the courtyard, hands locked between his knees, his eyes staring at the ground. He had refused food and had not responded to the attempts of others to talk to him. In fact, he had not spoken since his outburst after the landing. On the trek from the plane he had plodded along, head down, morose and fear-tensed, like a man walking from prison to gallows. He had not been hanged, and the surprise had sent him into a state of shock.

Id-Mar-Ok, having gotten the others into the cabins, sank down on the bench beside him.

"It has been a long day, has it not, Father?"

He grunted, but did not look up. She toyed with her *kay,* and after a pause tried again.

"Is it not nice to know that through all the devastation that man has wrought on our planet, the Moon remains the mistress of the night sky?"

He turned to face her, bewilderment in his sullen stare.

"The moon iss red, Miss," he mumbled gutturally, "and looks like it will burst apart in liddle pieces."

"Would you rather speak in the German language, Father?"

"Ugh. *Nein*—no. Rather I speak nodding."

With that, he lapsed into impenetrable shock. After a time, while the swollen red moon climbed toward the zenith, where it glared down upon the rim of equally angry volcanoes, the girl summoned Shur-Et-Na with her *kay.* The two of them plied their *kays* in unison, and when the shocked man slumped, they dragged him into a cabin and rolled him onto a pallet. Except for a guttural snore, he appeared to be inanimate. The Project Leader took away his clothing, as had been done with the others, and left instead colorless breech clouts and a blanket robe.

The garments they had given the women were softer, of gray and brown woollen cloth sparingly embroidered with bright-colored flowers, snakes and lizards. Nearly all possessions were taken from the recruits; the knitting bag was left to Osta, the diaper bag to Pretty Bean, as well as some clothing for her children. Hugh Shipsted was allowed to keep his wristwatch.

Crew members, relaxed in their loose robes, gathered around Shur-Et-Na in the courtyard after all the charges were locked in the huts to which they had been assigned. While the bloated moon soared to the zenith, the three men and the young woman conferred with long periods of mind-searching, with nods, shrugs and twinkling *kays.* The Leader was gratified that his daughter had been rescued and brought to him, but he was not happy about her. And he had grave misgivings about the remainder of the group. There was much explaining, crew members supporting each other. It had been necessary to locate others on the flight on which Osta had been booked. Some qualities of extrasensory perceptiveness had been necessary . . . Shur-Et-Na waved aside the explanations. By the time the moon had waned to a tired pink he had accepted the *fait accompli.*

At that point Gar-Na introduced a new subject that brought drooping heads up to defiant erectness. Ben-Ad tried to brush it away, while Id-Mar-Ok withdrew from the flaring argument with a weary shrug. The Project Leader, glaring angrily at his son, sheathed his *kay* and spoke aloud, biting off words with angry impatience.

"It has been decreed, my son. Neither prolonged discussion nor silly supplication can reverse the will of Oom. Even though we Project Leaders, by the grace of our great Divinity have been given some secrets of the universe, we are bound by honor that is stronger than the thread of our lives not to abuse them. We are of The People and must abide by the divine decrees for The People." He rose and regally drew his robe around him.

The younger man was not to be dismissed. Fire flashed from the stuttering *kay.*

Shur-Et-Na again spoke aloud, and more angrily than before. "We are not responsible for the moral lapses and the failures of Bov-No-Urr. By the imperium of the Nobles of Precious Blood he was chosen to head the Projects of Naz-Co, and if there be flaws in his character it is not our concern. Nor is it for us to emulate his mistakes, which have thrown gross shadows over future civilizations. It is rather for us to try to compensate for the cavortings of his monstrous progeny and kin who saved their ugly carcasses from death here and who went into the future to blasphemously call themselves gods."

He silenced Gar-Na's chattering *kay* with a wave of his hand. "I know. This poor clay you have brought along with my mentally deformed daughter can hardly be molded into gods worthy of the name. But we cannot risk our own dedicated lives, nor a precious *dzo*, to return them to their own time. We must ask the forgiveness of Oom for our shortcomings and give these miserable creatures an extra measure of devotion."

An uneasy groan far below the surface of the earth awakened the Project before sunrays had penetrated the banks of smoke and volcanic ash on the horizon. Around the courtyard metal utensils clattered to the ground and pottery danced behind the latticed barriers of shelves. Dog-like animals in the shrubbery set up dismal howls, and the creatures Smith had mistaken for goats emitted whimpering cries. Soon the recruits, terrified and articulate, were beating on the cottage doors.

Smith was first to be released, and "Bolly" talked to him earnestly while the settling shocks in the earth continued to keep clay vessels dancing and the animals crying. When the others were released, Brother Smith greeted them as host. He exuded confidence.

"Don't be alarmed, folks," he said as they gathered around. "Earthquakes are par for the course here—we have one 'most every morning before breakfast. But you can see they haven't done me any harm. I just take 'em in stride and go on about my business."

The passengers, not being able to find their clothes, had draped blankets around their shoulders. All except Hamilton, that is. He strutted naked into the center of the group when Smith finished speaking. Ella Pozniak, after a quick, horrified glance, ran back into a cottage; Vera Simpson forgot the quaking ground to stare. Pretty Bean was so busy with her babies that she didn't notice anything, and Nadine laughed hoarsely and moved to the side of the naked man. She tried to share her blanket with him, but he threw it aside, strutted and displayed his masculinity.

"When are you stupid jerks going to get it through your heads that we've been taken to the laundry—the brain laundry? This dog-nabbed ranch is nothing but a prison stockade. You all know you were locked in these little pens overnight, don't you?"

He proved to be a counter-irritant for the earthquake. The group forgot the buckling and weaving earth as they gathered around to stare and to listen to the naked man. Even the priest thrust his head out of the cabin, only to draw it back, turtle-like, when anyone looked his way. Brother Smith, feeling himself superfluous, went to his "goats." Pretty Bean and Joe Quail quieted the babies; Brock looked balefully at Nadine, while Hugh Shipsted's eyes sought "Tana."

The object of his quest soon hove into view carrying two earthenware jars of water suspended from a yoke on her shoulders. She weaved slightly, due to the heaving of the earth, but otherwise gave no heed to the quake. With a cry of dismay Hugh ran to her and tried to lift the burden from her shoulders.

"Darling, how could you— Why didn't you call me?"

She clung to the yoke. "Do you not understand, dear Hugh, this is woman's work? You must not degrade yourself in the eyes of other men." She drew her *kay* from a sleeve and toyed with it. "Why don't you get to the bathhouse ahead of the others? Gar-Na is there; he will show you how to dress yourself in our clothing." She pointed the *kay* and he moved off obediently.

Two other women, squat and swarthy, trotted up the incline, each carrying vessels that were larger than those on Id-Mar-Ok's yoke. Hugh passed them without seeing them. Id-Mar-Ok smiled wistfully after him as she sheathed her *kay*.

Hamilton continued to harangue the small circle around him. "Let's knock these goofy Reds on their arses and get ourselves back to that plane. You can count on your Uncle Laosy to get you out of here fast."

Curry, skilled at attracting attention, cleared his throat. Faces turned to him.

"This is absolutely preposterous! We have been taken in, fed and provided with shelter by the generous Brother Smith. He has lived up to his hospitable saying: his ranch is ours, indeed. You will notice that his servants have been thoughtfully instructed to take our clothing and shoes for cleaning—and didn't they need it, after that hike over the desert! It was a godsend that Brother Smith was with us on the plane, and it was an act of the good Lord Himself that we landed within walking distance of his ranch. The very least we can do is to volunteer to do some of the work around here."

"The stooge leading us to the slave-labor camp!" Hamilton bellowed. He swaggered over to Curry. "What do you get for your Judas work, High Pockets? An extra bowl of mush?"

Curry's eyes measured him calmly. "I'd advise you to get some kind of pockets . . ."

Hamilton spat. "Intellectual, that's what you are! Every damned double-dome from hell to breakfast is redder'n my great grandpa's undershirt. Fine bunch you are," he accused. "Isn't anybody with me?"

At that moment Osta, who had busied herself around the oven, whirled into the circle brandishing a heavy fire poker. She brought it down tellingly on Hamilton's head.

"We're all right here with you, Mister Dirty Name!"

The Laosian flyer crumpled to the ground unconscious and made a puddle of wet around himself.

Joe Quail and Pretty Bean laughed, others turned away, embarrassed, but Nadine lingered beside the fallen man long enough to drop her blanket over him. She dived naked into the nearest cottage.

Osta, standing over her fallen prey, raised her voice: "Gar-Na! Ben-Ad!" When the two men appeared she pointed to the collapsed Hamilton. "Drag this piece of trash out to the dump or t'row it to the wild dogs. I'm not going to have such filth around while I cook breakfast."

The men dragged the inert Hamilton to a cabin off to one side which was partially hidden in the shrubbery. There they laid him on a thin pallet and locket the door with their *kays*.

To open, doors slid upward into square, raised lintels that reared over the doorways like the false fronts of old Western saloons. All cottages were windowless, heated by the light that was mysteriously present in them and ventilated by louvered slits near the overhanging tile roofs. Sanitation was provided in an enclosed, closet-like area in each cabin through which a trough of running water passed. There were no mirrors, no clothes-hanging arrangements, no furnishings except the pallets, some straw-filled cushions for seating, and a long, coffin-like wooden chest in each cabin.

There was considerable grumbling over the fact that clothes and other possessions had been confiscated. Curry's bland explanations did not satisfy—perhaps did not satisfy him, even, but he clung doggedly to the myth of the Utah ranch.

Grumbling continued after everyone had been helped to bathe and dress in the clothing provided. The priest would not emrege from his cabin and, of course, Hamilton could not. After a morning meal of unlcavened cakes, unseasoned steamed roots, and unsweetened stewed berries, some of the group lingered at the table in the courtyard. Smith had gone to his "goats"; Curry, feeling the animosity toward him, had taken a walk; and Osta was with her father.

Nadine recalled Curry's statement about clothing. "It's us who have been taken to the cleaners. All our personal belongings and money gone . . ."

"What could we buy if we did have money?" Brock asked sullenly. "I could do with a razor."

"When your whiskers get long enough, you can pull 'em out, like I do," Joe Quail offered. "White people and all this fuss about shaving! If you're too chicken to pull out your whiskers, grow beards."

"I've got to do some laundry for the children," Pretty Bean complained. She looked longingly at the vessels of water the women had brought and left steaming on the top of the oven.

Vera Simpson bristled. "I think we're mighty ungrateful to Brother Smith, finding fault like this when he's sharing his food with us and offering us the best he has. After all, the Lord has scourged the earth with fire and brimstone . . ."

"Knock it off!" Nadine snarled. "Fire and brimstone notwithstanding, I need my avocado cream, my makeup, my shampoo, my girdle and my Sup-hose . . ."

Joe Quail laughed. "Don't forget your pretty britches that showed off your pretty behind."

Brock growled and half rose, but was prevented from doing battle by the appearance of Elsbeth. The little girl carried a *kay* thrust in front of her, and on the tip of it several leaves whirled like the propellers of an old-fashioned airplane.

"See, my great-father showed me—"

Osta ran out of a cabin and snatched up the girl. "It is time now for your bath and clean clothes."

"Will you make me a dolly out of straw?"

"I'll make you two dollies, but don't bother these people now."

Shur-Et-Na sauntered onto the scene.

"It is very distressing to learn that you have found our facilities inadequate. We have done the best we could with means at hand, and I hope you will bear with us. There are laundry facilities at the river—crude, but effective. There are preparations which some of our women use for their skin, laving oils and other vegetable preparations. I don't know much about these cosmetic things, but the girl you call Tana can give you the information. There's also a man around somewhere who knows how to remove beard painlessly."

"Gimme a razor of any kind and I'll shave myself," Brock muttered.

"There are no razors here," Shur-Et-Na informed him.

Joe Quail laughed insinuatingly. "That was easy to guess!"

Hugh Shipsted, who had not understood much of the conversation, rubbed smoothly shaven jaws. He did not remember how or where he had had his beard removed.

"Native Hawaiians are very clean people," he offered, "and gifted, too. I'm sure Tana can locate the man who shaved me . . ."

Joe Quail nudged him. "Wake up, farmer. We're in Utah, remember?"

Hugh pointed to a volcano that had begun to send up spurts of steam and lava. "That's Moana Loa. Don't you recognize it? It looks just like it does in pictures."

"I guess Brother Smith knows where we are!" Vera Simpson spoke as the missionary appeared.

"Uh, er, yeah, I guess so." He turned to Shur-Et-Na. "You've got to come quick, Bolly. Something awful bad's wrong with the goats. Their hooves have gone soft."

"Don't worry, Misser Smith," the older man said soothingly as he led the missionary away. "It happens about this time every year. I guess you've never noticed it before."

Chapter XI

Group Two

Dr. Laura Lindholm pirouetted to model the full-skirted, embroidery-trimmed dress she had been given.

"If the people who did this work are the 'culturally deprived' tribes whom we've been brought here to elevate, I think we'd better go back to our own ghettos. Just look at this exquisite handwork!"

"Stitches so even they might have been made by machine," Dr. Phillope Applebaum commented dryly.

"No machine could knot thread like that . . ."

"Didn't know you were a home crafts expert, Laura," Dr. Vaughn Wright offered.

"I'm not, but—"

"Your Tibetan creation, or wherever you think it's from, might have been turned out in lots of a thousand each in a New Jersey factory."

Dr. Irma Boyd, who had been studying designs on the pottery bowls in which their morning meal had been served, looked up.

"There's something of the Chaldean about these figures. If only I'd been permitted to bring along some of my references. It may be that we are in a pocket of lost civilization. Perhaps it's because the tribes here don't conform to the Cultural Revolution that they must be re-educated."

"Right now I'd like to have my own clothes and a shave," Dr. Emory-Leonard complained. "Most uncomfortable night on that creaking straw thing. I'm sure there were bugs in it. I feel like I'd been bitten all over."

"Our host—what was his name, Bovna?—certainly could have been more specific about what's expected of us."

"I think his name is Bovnurr," McMillan put in. No one paid any attention to him.

"The square lintels, the sled runners, and the peculiar footwear of these people—yes, I'm sure it's something that goes back at least to the Chaldean . . . It may well be that we'll be the students instead of the instructors."

"You want to get us shot?" Wright asked.

"Oh, come now," Dr. Markham chided. "We're jumping to altogether too many conclusions. In the first place, we don't know that we've reached our destination; in the second, we don't know the nature of the people to be instructed. And thirdly, we must remember that the term 'culturally deprived' covers a very broad spectrum. The fact that people do beautiful hand embroidery and use sleds with curled-up runners doesn't indicate they are not intellectually backward. I'm sure you will all agree that handcrafts of an advanced nature and the most abysmal superstitions often go together. Isolation caused by either geographical or political barriers provides the *milieu* for the development of handcraft, yet at the same time permits the perpetuation of primitive beliefs. For instance, the serpent that is coiled on Dr. Applebaum's breast—"

"Eeee!" Phillope Applebaum squealed before she realized that Dr. Markham referred to the embroidery on the bodice of her dress.

Others laughed, but Dr. Markham continued without giving notice to the interruption. "The serpent we see here is adorned with plumes about its head. That—and I believe our Doctor of Theology here will agree—indicates the deification of the serpent."

McMillan nodded absently. "Perhaps you're right, Dr. Markham, but I lean toward a different hypothesis. Adding up the sum of the earthquake this morning, plus the existence of what appear to be cinders, plus the plumed serpent motif, I'd be inclined to say—"

"*Non sequitur*, Dr. McMillan!" Markham countered irritably. "That's the trouble with you theologians, you've lost the power of deductive reasoning! We have over here a fact—an unassailable truth, if you will: we were approached and abducted, lured away, kidnapped—whatever you want to call it—by our friends the Chin-coms for the purpose of assisting them in raising the cultural level of some of their subjects . . ."

"Hear! Hear! Hear!" Emory-Leonard, Wright, Boyd and Applebaum applauded.

"Solid fact," Emory-Leonard summed up.

"We were brought somewhere in an aircraft," Markham continued, his face suffused with dark blood. "By all possible standards of reasoning, we are somewhere in Asia—somewhere within the territory of our Chinese friends. We are in a desert; it is logical to assume that it is some part of the Gobi!" He was screaming now, his face purple.

Dr. Lindholm and Dr. McMillan exchanged knowing glances.

"There's only one thing wrong with that fine bit of reasoning, Dr. Markham," Laura Lindholm offered, but was not allowed to continue.

"Nothing wrong with the reasoning, nothing I tell you!" Emory-Leonard screamed. "We're in the Gobi, the Gobi, the Gobi!"

"Earthquakes, volcanoes, cinders, Southern Hemisphere constellations," McMillan summed up. "We're probably on one of the moons of Jupiter!"

Irma Boyd opened her mouth, but did not speak. A man who might have been a rough copy of Markham stepped into the clearing. He was somewhat taller than Markham, straighter, darker and beardless, but he had the same self-satisfied bearing and the same condescending manner. He looked around the circle like a professor making one of his rare appearances before a class.

"For the benefit of those who were sleeping late this morning, may I introduce myself. I am your Project Leader, Bov-No-Urr; the name is Nascan, meaning the son of failing light. I have all my life tried to—how would say it in your idiom?—live it down. We are here at an oasis at the edge of the great Gobi Desert . . ."

He allowed time for Markham to gloat.

". . . We are here at this place we call Naz-Co in our local dialect, for the purpose of receiving some basic training to enable you, my worthy guests, to go as gods among a primitive people, about whom you will be told more. For the time being, we will concern ourselves with such mundane affairs as the selection and preparation of vegetable foods. We are not going to take up hunting or the killing of game, because it is my plan that you shall go as apostles of gentleness, that you will lead as the great Gautama led, by example. But enough of the vision for now, my worthies.

"Today, the women will go with my daughter and worthy colleague, Y-Stan-Urr, to learn the preparation of fibers for making cloth . . ."

A sullen, dark young woman, unusually tall and square-shouldered, stepped out of nowhere to take her place beside the Project Leader. She did not smile or look with any interest at any of the group.

"We men," Bov-No-Urr continued, "will go to the fields to learn the cultivation of the *glig.*"

The young woman drew a *kay* from a sleeve, touched her father's shoulder. He whirled around to face her, angrily, so it appeared. Then he drew his own *kay* and they communicated furiously for a moment.

He turned back to the astonished and waiting group. "My apologies, friends, for this impolite 'deaf and dumb' speech which we have developed in this isolated area. My daughter advises me that a bathhouse is much more important to us now than *glig* for our tables. That lesson will come later."

As he spoke, the two attendants who had hauled baggage from the aircraft to the oasis appeared and stood impassively awaiting a signal from the Project Leader.

Dr. McMillan edged closer to Laura Lindholm. "I still don't believe it's the Gobi," he whispered.

"I don't know what it is," she answered guardedly. "But I know what it is not—it is not kosher."

Chapter XII

The meeting of Osta Eisen and Gerda Mayer erupted in spontaneous combustion. The older woman, frail, graying and bent, was almost pummeled to pieces in her daughter's joyous embraces. There had never been but one love in Osta's life, and that was for *Mutter*. Wilbur Eisen had been a necessary nuisance—a girl must have a suitor and eventually a husband and father for her children. The daughters were toys at first, then, as they grew up to have minds of their own, they became annoying. But in Osta's eyes, her angelic *Mutter* was not besmirched with human failing. The homely changeling daughter not only worshipped the only parent she had known, she made a ritual of performing her chores in exactly the way *Mutter* had taught. The teachings of Gerda Mayer, which had helped to bring the Sudeten community in which she lived through a crisis, were to Osta holy writ.

In the 1920's when the twin curses of inflation and indemnities were grinding the farmers and working people of the Homeland into abject poverty, Gerda Mayer taught her neighbors long-forgotten crafts that helped them to self-sufficiency and more comfortable living. Hence, Osta would permit no deviation from *Mutter*'s teachings. For that reason the Eisen Bohemian Home Bakery followed literally the advertising slogan it carried in Gothic script over the door: "Like Mother Used to Bake." In Germany in the 1920's *Mutter* baked her breads and pastries from grain that was grown without chemical fertilizer, that was hand cut, home threshed, stone ground and mixed by hand in a home-made stoneware vessel. Forty and fifty years later, Osta insisted on following the same procedure to produce her bakery goods in Chicago, even though it meant traversing long distances between farm and mill and bakery and scouting the necessary ingredients over four states. When Wilbur Eisen tried to cut corners by using "boughten" flour for some of the products, he died soon after he had sampled, as was his custom, the first of a morning's batch of blueberry muffins. In Osta's mind, his death was fitting punishment for his violations of the ritual.

Now, united with the mother whose memory she had worshipped for many years, her emotion burst all bonds. She laughed and cried and flailed the old woman with her well-muscled arms. She picked her up and cradled her; she set her down and danced with her; she kissed her, entwined her fingers in the silky white hair, and hugged the frail woman until her ribs threatened to crack. While

Gerda was overjoyed to see her daughter, she was more contained.

Osta's teary apologies mingled with her whoops and squeals of joy. She was sorry she had been rough, but on such an occasion how could one resist expending all one's bottled-up energy? Gerda expended her energy to the fullest, also. Words in the German language became entangled with plunging thoughts. No complete sentences were formed and no facts established. Osta knew that *Mutter* was alive; she was here in this strange place; she had been rescued from the violence that had swept the Homeland, as Osta had been rescued from nuclear destruction.

At length they quieted sufficiently to seat themselves on cushions that were scattered around the floor of the sparsely furnished cabin. More soberly, they exchanged a few lucid sentences, the older woman toying with a *kay* and using it here and there for emphasis. She asked a few questions about her granddaughers and the great-grandchild whom Osta had brought with her. She memorized their names and asked to see Elsbeth soon. Questions Osta asked were parried, but in her excitement she did not notice that her mother had told her nothing.

Before long, *Vater* returned, and there followed a mind-to-mind consultation between the parents in which Gerda used the *kay* with almost as much dexterity as did Shur-Et-Na. Osta extracted some facts from the conversation that excluded her, as a child does when elders attempt to talk over his head.

"All right now," she interrupted, speaking in the language with which she had become familiar, "before you spill any more of the secrets you don't want me to learn, just tell me what everybody knew at home, how *Mutter* goes an innocent girl for a walk into the woods one morning, and in the evening of the same day she comes back puffed up seven months with me."

Shur-Et-Na gracefully folded his long length onto a cushion. He answered his daughter in the English she had spoken, which, it was plain, Gerda understood—either the spoken words or thoughts as the words were spoken.

"I met your mother in a clearing in the woods," he

said simply. "We were attracted to each other instantly, and I brought her back to my home here in the *dzo* I was flying. That is, a plane like the one in which you came here. We went through a ceremony of marriage here at Naz-Co, and you were conceived in the natural course of events. But before you were born it was necessary for your mother to return to her home in order to carry out work for which she had been trained. According to the plan we then followed, people brought here for training during that world crisis were returned to their locations on the same day they were taken. Do you now understand, Osta-Na?"

Osta, who had moved restlessly around the small, bare room while her father spoke, sank to the floor with a spanking thud and fumbled with her knitting.

"*Ja, ja,* the *where* part I understand, the *how* I know about, but it's the *when* part that won't go through this thick skull. It is all so crazy. You told me when first we talked, *Vater,* that you couldn't come to my birth bed because then you had been dead for fifty t'ousand years, but here you are as alive as I am. Do you mean that in this place when you're dead you don't stay dead?"

The parents exchanged glances. Gerda refused to undertake the explanation.

Shur-Et-Na chose his words carefully. "You see, dear daughter, Time is a great, invisible sphere. As the Earth is round, so the Universe is round, and Time surrounds it, like atmosphere surrounds the Earth. Do you understand?"

Osta counted stitches a moment. "*Ja,* I understand the words. But how did I get over here in Time, if I was rooted down over there in Time?"

"That, my dear Osta-Na, is a secret brought to this planet long ago by some creatures whom we call The People. The Great Chart of the Universe, plus the magnetics that cancel gravity and the full use of mental energy—all things which The People of Precious Blood taught their descendants—enable us to travel through the Time layers around the Universe. Perhaps you were awakened, or stirred, when the *dzo* passed through the Blue Belt. In your body, which will not be born for fifty thousand years, you and the others with you entered Time at one point, and thanks to the skilled navigation of Ben-

Ad and perfect coordination and ability of Gar-Na, you came out here—fifty thousand years, give or take a few years, before the time you lived on Earth. You were brought here, to a place that exists only as a faint memory on the Earth of your time."

Again Osta counted stitches. "Then the pull-over I make for Ruth takes me fifty t'ousand years. Is that what you tell me?"

Shur-Et-Na nodded. "Except, dear Osta, and this is a hard fact with which you must live, there will be no Ruth to wear it when it is finished."

"You don't, then, take me back to *when* I was?"

"It is not possible, Osta, dear. We could return you to the time you were taken on board the *dzo,* but not *before* that time. And I'm sure you realize that you were taken off the Earth on the day that all life—most of it—was wiped from it."

"*Ja,* I guess I know that."

Osta tucked the knitting into the bag and sat staring into space. Tears trickled from her eyes; she sniffed a few times, then mopped her face with the skirt of her dress.

"If Gar-Na had asked me what I want to do, when he came to me at the jetport by the weighing station, I think I would take this—to have my grandmother and my mother and my father and to know about my birthing. *Ja*—" She smiled at her parents, who were waiting tensely for her reaction. "I think I choose this."

Gerda ran to her and hugged her, and Shur-Et-Na put his long arms around both of them.

Osta broke the embrace. "It is time now I start the fire to make supper, but some quick words, maybe."

"You want to know *why*. Is that it, my daughter?" Gerda asked.

"*Ja*—why? You don't make this big thing and send Gar-Na and the others fifty t'ousand years, and collect others, too, just to save my ugly skin. No, you've got some big plan yet. Can you tell quick so supper will be on time?"

The tall man laughed and gestured with his *kay* to Gerda. She kissed her daughter, threw a shawl around her shoulders, and started out.

"I will get the slaves started on the evening meal, as I

have been doing for a long time. We have no clocks here, but the sun rises and sets, and we get hungry and sleepy, just like in other times."

Shur-Et-Na seated himself again. "I cannot tell you all of the *why* that you and the others are here, Osta-Na. That is one of the things you must learn along with the others."

"You mean you will try to teach those dumbheads something? That woman with the put-on face that wants to sleep with every man there is, that girl with two bastards yet and one more coming, and that black-faced Indian who hates all the white people? Only the old man with the black hat is any good, and maybe the priest."

"Please try not to judge them, my dear. If my crew had had to find perfect people for this Project, I'm afraid they would have been lost in the world disaster, as well as you. When we deal with human beings, we must start with the imperfect, as The People did long ago to teach us what little we know.

"First, my dear Osta, I must ask that you let those who will continue to, believe they are on Brother Smith's ranch in Utah. That is part of the plan, and since you are my helper, you must do this.

"Secondly, we will live for a time on a day-to-day basis. The teaching is in the living, and vice versa. If you remember, that is the way your beloved mother taught the people of her Homeland.

"You can take over some of your mother's work here. We live in a world without grocery stores, dress shops, plumbing and electric gadgets. You know how to do that and by doing it you will be teaching the others."

"I can do the things my mother taught me. But I don't know if I can make these clucks learn anything. The disaster was good enough for such people—lazy women sitting around all day gawping at the brainwashing machine, letting their kids run wild and have candy and carbonated drinks and feeding their families old boughten foods put up with embalming fluid! I tried to tell people—I talked till my tongue was black and ready to drop out yet, even my own girls called me crazy and went out and bought long-handler mops to wash the floors!"

The old man laughed at his daughter's outburst. "All

that has been remedied, Osta, my dear. I'm sure you know well enough how to cure meat and to winnow out grain, but that is not all we want our recruits to learn. You remember that while your mother was showing the farmers how to raise better crops and livestock and to cure the meat and grind the grain, she was also inspiring them to admire the china-painting, the embroidery, the fine weaving and other beautiful things. It was your Homeland, I believe, that excelled in making some of the world's most beautiful figurines, and weaving the most exquisite patterns of cloth."

"You mean you think those old useless things are good, too?"

"That I do, my dear daughter. The man who knows no more than animal existence is an animal; he is reaching for the stars when he can look up from his plow to admire a passing butterfly."

"Hmn." Osta repacked her knitting.

"I want you, dear Osta-Na, to learn the butterfly part of existence. Will you try?"

Osta regarded her father somewhat sadly. "While you were making a child, my father, you should have made one with butterfly wings, not these sow-ears I've got!"

Chapter XIII

The Diary

Many loves hath a Sun,
Whilst females of the realm,
Lonely orbs, pale moons,
Each hath but one.

So ran a little verse (or my translation of it) which I learned in girlhood in the great cold halls of my clan's educational building. It was directed to those of us who were beginning to feel the first flutters of interest in our male cousins or the young men who came and went around us. Our instructress, innocent of face and not much older than we were, explained that the male must make his own solar system with mates in number to revolve around him, serving his appetites and whims, while they, in turn, warmed themselves in his resplendence, drawing strength from his strength and life from his life.

A man took wives in accordance with his physical needs, his clan standing—which by our customs signified his wealth—and for the purpose of cementing clan ties. Therefore, a man with many wives could rise high in the politics of his clan and live in splendor. It was a great honor for a woman to be taken into a household of ten, fifteen, or even twenty wives. My own was a ten-wife home. We lived in a mansion of carved stone and were served by many slaves, eating the choicest of refined foods and wearing the finest of embroidered woolens. Women occupied themselves with poetry, music, and weaving, while their children were nursed by slaves.

Nevertheless, I girlishly dreamed of a marriage which would remain forever in the state of beginning—or "honeymoon," according to the idom of this language. I wanted to be the sole object of my mate's attention, the only mother of his children. One after another I refused marriage prospects who were brought before me. My father was patient and did not command me to marry. He realized that forced matrimony is a source of great unhappiness in a household. Other wives resented one who did not love their husband, and the man soon tired of a woman whose favors were not freely given. She might even be left childless, a condition no woman wants to face.

My rebellion against the formalized traditions of the Precious Blood aristocracy took shape at the height of my rather stormy adolescence. It was then that I learned about the Projects which were underway in the Valley of the Naz, to the north and west of our home. In fact, a distant cousin—with whom I was expected to mate—had given his life to Project work, and it was he who told me about them. I liked Ben-Ad, enjoyed exchanging thoughts with him, but he was only a friend, not a resplendent Sun around which I would be content to orbit for the rest of my life. The idea of the Projects was based upon the great idealism of our mythical forebears, or as it had been interpreted. The thought of implanting our culture in peoples who were wallowing in the mud of ignorance, so to speak, inflamed my young mind; it uplifted my troubled spirit and drew off the emotional poisons which had made me miserable. Before consulting my family, I struck kays *with Ben-Ad, which sealed my promise to give my life to that work.*

When I made my announcement at a ceremonial family gathering, my father, brothers, uncles, brothers-in-law, and male cousins, with no deference to etiquette, burst simultaneously into violent protest. Their eyes blazed, and I am sure that sparks flew from the kays *that they plied so vigorously. Later, in the Lounge of Women, the* kays *of my mother, half-mothers, sisters, and sisters-in-law flew just as furiously. It was unthinkable, improper, unmaidenly; it obscured my chances of matrimony. What was most important, it would cut me off from my family at a time when all families, especially those of Precious Blood, should be drawing closer together to meet a doom which was rushing toward us.*

Ben-Ad, who wanted very much to take me to the Naz-Co Project, explained patiently, resorting to the use of his voice now and then, that the Projects were in accordance with the wishes of our ancestors whose blood was more precious than our own, that they were but an extension of the beginning of our race on Earth when those saintly First Ones came to the raw planet to implant the Flame of Oom. If we believed, as all of us were taught, that the beginning had been part of the plan of our great and all-powerful god, we must also believe that it was our sacred duty to carry the Flame beyond our own time. Our world was soon to die, to go down into nothingness in flame and flood because of the errant red moon. Was it not our sacred duty to use to our utmost the knowledge and skill we had developed in order to carry forward into other dark times the Flame of Oom? The workers in the projects at Naz-Co were evangelists of time. Our interference in the lives of certain selected individuals in future times was in the sacred cause, and those who worked at implanting the Flame of Oom in the recruits brought to Naz-Co would attain a nobility of spirit higher than the mere nobility of blood.

In spite of Ben-Ad's eloquent defense of the Projects,

the argument lasted for four days of a five-day Harvest Festival. The time of merrymaking for the Ok-Nokken Clan was spent in quarrel-making. We were all weary from clashing wills and tearing thoughts from each other's minds. At last my father lifted his kay *to forbid my going; Ben-Ad raised his to release me from my vow. The women pressed around to gloat at the kill, so to speak*

At that moment an earthquake hit. It disrupted thought, extinguished the electronic light with which our mansion was lit, jarred the building and its foundation, and whitened us all with loosed alabaster. It was not a serious quake. No building stones came down to crush us, no fissures opened near us, and no volcanoes spewed lava on us. But it served to remind the sobered Ok-Nokkens that our time was short and that the will of Oom could not be altered with a flick of the kay.

Standing ghost-whitened in the darkened hallway I raised my kay.

"Hereby I relinquish my place in this family; I give up my pleasures of weaving and embroidering ceremonial robes, of painting sacred symbols on unfired clay and cultivating plants for their flowers. I am laying aside my beautiful embroidered robes, and in garments of the lowest caste I shall set forth for the Place of Projects in order to do the work of Oom, who has spoken by earthquake and thunder."

The room was still. The light came on. My father lowered the kay *he had held rigidly aloft, and we shook the white dust from ourselves.*

"There is one day left for merriment," my mother said by voice.

We celebrated, making the most of that short time to recall the amusing little things which had happened among us, to sing the songs we loved, to tease and playfully berate each other—and to forget that tomorrow our bones would lie in watery graves.

On the brassy morning when the new year started, I put on garments such as those worn by slaves, and with scant provisions and no possessions other than my kay *and a change of clothing, I set out on foot. Part of the renunciation and vow was the promise to leave one's home on foot.*

There was nothing in the vow which required that one should walk all the way to Naz-Co, however. The Projects would not have been able to function if those who worked in them had been forced to walk through vast reaches of dangerous swamp and jungle and over the wind-punished escarpments that were so high that hearts often stopped when the climbers neared the summits.

I climbed a tortuous path to the plateau where Ben-Ad and a companion had landed their time-traveling dzo. *It was there I met Shur-Et-Na, who was later to head the project on which I worked. At that time he was teamed with my cousin to take the* dzo *through the Blue Belt of Time.*

Perhaps it is well to explain here that recruits brought to Naz-Co through the magnetic hub of Time were put into a state of hypnosis, and kept in that state to the point where we could induce them to believe they were experiencing something rather ordinary. This led to complications, and it was the task of Project workers to handle the situations as they arose. The things we taught in the Projects cannot be implanted in minds that are disturbed over strange surroundings. Also, it is essential that we embed most of our teachings in the emotional, rather than the thinking, centers of the mind.

Needless to say, there have been many heartbreaking failures, particularly among the recruits in the Projects under the direction of Bov-No-Urr, under whom I worked at first. It was the contention of Shur-Et-Na that Bov-No-Urr was bringing in the wrong type of recruit, in that he insisted upon getting persons of standing in their own communities and professions—the artists, the scientists, the political leaders and so on. These people, almost invariably, could not accept the final, full-awareness, stage of the indoctrination. Some broke out of the hypnotism and could not accept what they discovered; others could not accept the revelation made to them before they were given assignments. Madness resulted, and generally death followed soon. It is true that Shur-Et-Na has had greater success, but the danger faces us, too. For instance, the discovery that Brother Smith made about the soft feet of the gurs, *which disrupted his belief that the animals were the goats on his Utah ranch in the twentieth century, can* cause major trouble on the present project. As a matter of fact, each of these recruits in which we have placed our greatest hope presents some sort of special problem.

Those problems are for other entries, however. Now I must resolve my own problem. I am in love, a condition I have never before considered. For the first time I have heard—or felt is a better word—the promptings of an inner voice. In his presence I hear the song of the ginga as it meets its mate of a lifetime; I hear the harps of high mountain peaks in the wind; I experience the joy of the mother gur as she nuzzles her first cub, and of the ageing mother whose favorite son returns from a mission of great danger. For the first time I feel that I am truly needed and that at last life has taken on a meaning.

At first, Hugh's simple mind baffled me. Never had I encountered one of such remarkable simplicity. To him, the course of life was a straight line from birth to death. The sun rose, warmed the fields, rains came, corn grew. One worked, one accepted the teachings of parents and instructors; one conformed and sought to remain obscure. And love was a thing of constancy, directed first to mother and then to mate, not to be transferred or diluted by thoughts of any but the one chosen to step into the place of mother. Tana was the love object and would so remain, in the terms of his devout thinking, "till death do us part." I was Tana, and Hugh loved me with undying devotion.

On the bus when I directed a spurt of kinetic energy toward him in order to put him under temporary hypnosis, he identified me as his Tana. Since then, there has been no need for applied hypnosis; he has hypnotized himself, and may never recover from the one delusion that I am Tana. He wants me to wed with him, to become his one wife and one mother for his children. The greatest wish of my whole life has been laid as a gift at my feet.

Furthermore, my desire for him as a mate draws me with a force stronger than that which lifts a dzo and sends it whirling into space-time. Yet there are heavy drags on my soaring wishes. Can I tie my life to one whose mind is not as developed as that of a humble slave? Thinking of my own people, whose minds soar like the dzo, whose thoughts can be birdsong, sunrise, a volcanic storm or the whir of massive machinery, I am aware of the great *loneliness I must bear. With whom can I share the joys and the pains of spirit? With whom can I communicate the great visions that assail one when passing through the Blue Belt of Time? The caress of lips to lips, hand to hand, or body to body cannot compensate for the lack of that magnificent touch of mind to mind in great thought. Must the forfeit of that joy be the price I must pay for my girlhood wish?*

Also, there is family honor. Do I have the courage to face my family again, as I did when I took my vow of renunciation for the Projects, and tell them I have decided to go ig-saki? *Forgiveness was granted when they became convinced that I was going to serve a noble cause. But to tell them I am deserting them and the Project in these last days of our existence is indeed another matter.*

"There is a time for living and a time for dying," my father said when he had heard all my faltering confession.

He remained for a hundred heartbeats crumpled forward on his cushion, face in his hands. They were noble hands, untouched by labor in the fields or shops, and in the veins that throbbed under the ageing, transparent skin ran the blood of those who had come to Earth from the dying planet of a red star. The nobility of that blood carried with it the weight of obligation, and my father had fulfilled that obligation to the best of his ability. Not only did I love his face and form; I loved his courage and his strength.

"No, Id-Mar," he said by voice as he raised his tortured face. It was a fine face by the standards of any race of which I knew, deep gray-brown eyes well spaced beside the thin, straight nose, forehead high and broad, neither bulging nor recessive, and a chin that buttressed the profile line with strength but did not dominate. From his comeliness I have inherited what is sometimes called beauty, although the dark cast of my mother's more lowly people shows in my skin.

"No," he repeated, emphasizing the edict with his kay. *"When it comes time for the mass death that has been decreed by Oom, you will be here among us, with me, my ten wives, thirty-two other children and their wives and husbands, and their many children. The Ok-Nokken Clan will be together in that last cleansing moment of our race."*

"But, Father," I pleaded, "I must return to the Project to fulfill my obligation there. Those of Precious Blood," I reminded him, "do not violate sacred vows."

"Of course you must go," he was quick to agree. "But when this consignment of recruits has been dispatched, you will return here to take part in the death-awaiting ceremonies we have planned." He raised his kay to cut off my protest.

"The Project on which you are now working will be the last," he informed me. "The nobles of all clans of Precious Blood met in Continental Conclave recently and came to that decision. It would be heartless to bring other recruits to Naz-Co for a ten-tal training period only to have them devoured by lava or by the lava-heated waves that will soon wash over the continent. Our formal decree will be carried to Shur-Et-Na and Bov-No-Un on the dzo which will return you to Naz-Co and which will bring you back here when this project ends."

So saying, he walked proud and straight to his sanctum. I believe he knew, as I knew, that we would never see each other again, but he did not turn or lift his kay in farewell. Nor did I cry out or run after him, as I longed to do. For a hundred heartbeats I stood in the hall of my tomb-like home where all but my father and I slept, and the weight of grief that tumbled down on me was as crushing as the weight of the heavy carved stones that would soon crush the bodies of those I loved. Yet even then in that moment of black gloom a hope was forming, like the seed of life taking root in the womb of a woman.

The mute dzo pilot permitted me to sit beside him in the flight compartment where the dawn view was unrestricted. We flew low enough to see many particulars of the dark terrain below. Circling over the vast cordillera I shuddered at the fissures that gaped like suppurating wounds, and the spills of molten lava that coursed like bright blood downward, devouring mining and metal-working installations, villages and farmlands. We were close enough to see ant-like lines of homeless refugees picking their way down the lava-strewn slopes. They were my fellow countrymen, many of them related through Precious Blood, and I felt as though I were walking with them, tossed by the violently quaking earth, terrified, yet *clinging to life as they clung to the precipitous mountain-sides. Soon they would be engulfed by the hungry waves that were raging over plains below to hiss hotly and send up great spumes of steam as they met the river of lava. For the first time I comprehended the nature of the doom that was rushing toward us. Not only the people and their puny homes and mines and factories and fields were to be destroyed, but the very land beneath us: our mountains and rivers and plains would be reduced to the swampy slime of Beginning. All this was irrevocably decreed by Oom. Only the cowardly ones of animal blood would misuse the special secret of Time travel to extend their unworthy lives.*

Our divine guide had decreed that a few areas of the Earth's surface would survive the onslaught of water and molten rock. One of these was the high plateau above the Vally of the Naz, and on this our wise forebears had laid out the master chart of Time, space and Earth surfaces. The Great Chart with its lines of intricate calculations carefully executed with alabaster-dipped stones was to be preserved for eons to come. It was intact but dim at the time of the nearly total destruction of the Earth in the twentieth century. Gar-Na had skimmed over it to take homeward guidance from its marvelously straight lines that stretched for a sight-length across the gray-white desert on the southern continent.

Part of the noble obligation of those consecrated to work in the Projects and to die at the time of the swollen red moon was to keep the precious lines of the Chart free from cinders and falling debris while destruction roared over the rest of the world. It was decreed by Oom that the most noble of these would leave their bones along the lines of the Chart. Stooped slaves were now carefully sweeping the long lines of precisely placed white stones.

As we plummeted down toward the cleanly-marked Naz-Co plateau I marveled again at the genius and fore-sight and dedication of our great ancestors. Had they, I asked myself, given their hopes, their skills, and even their substance to found a race of men that would accept finality? Were the nobles of attenuated Precious Blood forgetting the strength of the vision that had brought them into being?

The first feeble streamers of clouded sunlight touched the markings on the plateau as we landed. By that time the seed of hope that had taken root as my father walked away from me was assuming shape.

Chapter XIV

Id-Mar-Ok

Looking down at the Place of Projects as they came in for a landing, Id-Mar-Ok felt that she was seeing it for the first time. Naz-Co was located in a deep cut that ran through the plateau, beginning at the foot of the cordillera as a tree of fine little branches. Beyond the protective barriers of the mountains the ocean had gone wild, like a bed of mad serpents. Some writhed angrily almost to the mountaintops, hissing their threats of destruction. The Naz River winked here and there from the bottom of the basalt defile, then spilled out like liquid moonlight into a great salt marsh that hugged the base of the plateau.

The Naz-Co complex consisted of four octagon clusters of *dimds,* or cabins. (English words were replacing the short guttural ones of The People in the girl's mind when she tethered her thoughts with the words of languages.) The clusters were made up of octagon-shaped cabins that surrounded a central utility courtyard. Each octagon was flanked by precisely set four-sided shell buildings for slave quarters, and spaced between the clusters were rectangular fields, so that from above one could read the pattern of Everlasting Vigilance, the motif that appeared in stone-carvings, in cloth woven for temple use, and on the parchment one inscribed with prayer. Silently and with soaring thought Id-Mar-Ok renewed the vow she had taken to keep alive forever the ascending Flame of Oom, beyond the doom that was rushing in angry waters and spurting lava to destroy her world, beyond the great excrescence of the twentieth century from which would fall the murderous burning snow, and beyond the time when the Sun would grow red and the planet Earth would cool. To the Maker of the Universe with its encircling Blue Belt of Time, "forever" meant beyond a thousand planetary and solar doomsdays.

The sunrise sky was frigid blue, and frost glistened from the craggy volcanic cliffs as Id-Mar-Ok and the *dzo* pilot made their way by *gur*-sled from the landing field down into the valley. They followed a much shorter route than the one taken with the recruits. Hardy moss peeped from beneath a layer of pumice, and a host of brilliantly colored birds fluted in the dew-touched ferns. Flowering shrubs that lined the path dipped laden branches as if paying homage to the young woman of Precious Blood. Frilled lilies of many hues swam in the stagnant water of *tana,* or sewage, ponds, disguising the odors of offal with their cloying perfume.

Two lines of sturdy slave women carried urns of water and baskets of food on their heads, making their way from the river and the storage caves near it to the hearths of the Projects that were in operation.

Id-Mar-Ok alighted from the sled at the hidden temple cluster, which from the height of clouds looked like the others in the complex, but which was constructed of stones carved in sacred designs and was actually one building instead of eight, with courtyard simulated on the roof. This had been done for protection in the event non-believers should learn the secret of *dzo* flight and wish to harm the edifice of worship. She paused beside the building and lifted her face to greet the shafts of sunlight that shot through the serrations of the eastern mountains. She felt the warmth of the Flame within her, and she hummed a few bars of the Morning Hymn, which was playing softly within the temple; then she went to her quarters to prepare for the day.

Ella Pozniak
"Nein!"

Osta, with upraised oven paddle, dived across the courtyard to snatch a bowl of congealed turtle fat from

Ella, who was about to give it to the wild dogs that crowded up, yapping, to the edge of the clearing.

"Good fat is not for the dogs! Into the soap-making crock it must go. How do you think we get the soap to wash our dirty clothes and our dirty selves?"

Ella, who had lost much of her timidity in the sixty days at "Brother Smith's ranch," cowered before the strident and domineering Osta. She was cornered between the angry woman and the snarling, fox-faced animals who had been maddened by the smell of food.

"I didn't know," she stammered tearfully. "No one ever told me about soap-making."

"How could a woman so dumb as you live so long! Did you think soap grows on trees, maybe?"

One of the animals leaped at Osta, seized her robe, and began to chew a spot impregnated with the grease. She beat it away with the paddle and whacked about the bushes until all the animals had fled.

"No good chowhounds! Not once do they bark at robbers who come at night to steal our food, and no good are they for children's pets! I tell my *Vater* not once but fifty times he must get rid of them . . ." She eyed the other woman speculatively.

"How you like a new coat?"

"Well, er—" Ella hesitated. "I was going to buy a new one when I got to Honolulu, one with a wide collar, like they're wearing."

"Right here I think you've got the collar, and the coat we make from some of that good woollen we've been weaving."

"Where would you get the pro-lon lining?"

"Is it a coat you want, or the world to be like it is not any more?"

Ella, her face sagging in thought, looked at Osta for a long moment, then swept the scene with inquiring eyes. The "ranch" had disappeared like a desert mirage, and she found herself in a strange place, as one did in dreams. The garments she wore were strange, including the turn-up-toed moccasins. A wave of dizziness swept over her, and she sat down heavily on a bench.

The other woman, mistaking her vertigo for anger, touched her gently on the shoulder.

"You must excuse please my sometimes rough ways. It is hard for me to understand women who don't know about all these things like soap-making from rendered fat and wood ashes, and making a coat from animal skins. They come natural to me, but I don't know about things like making music and painting, like you and Vera do. Maybe we make a bargain: I teach you how to make soap and you teach me some of the 'butterfly' things you know."

"Well, maybe . . ."

Ella withdrew into her shell. It was all so unbelievable, like a psychedelic trip. Maybe it was. But was she starting on it, or recovering from it? The cliffs across the little river, which had been chalk-white, were now a kind of purplish brown with cracks in them and places where the rocks from above had spilled through breaks. They were more livable as landscapes go, but were they real? She thought of Brother Smith, who had been taken away because he thought his goats' feet had gone soft, and wondered if they'd take her away, also.

For some time she had felt that things weren't just right. There were strange sounds at night, like music or singing in a foreign tongue, very low and soft. If one woke up and listened, the sounds skittered away, like night creatures slinking back into the woodwork. She knew she hadn't imagined this, because both Pretty Bean and Vera had mentioned it. One could understand a pregnant woman having strange fancies, but no Oak Park slumlord could be deceived by crickets or singing mice.

The stewardess, Tana, came up and spoke to the German woman, waving her bright wand as she did so. Ella heard her words clearly.

"Were the dogs annoying you?" she asked.

After a slight pause the odd German woman answered what she must have thought she heard instead of the spoken words.

"Ja, ja," she nodded. "My mother takes care of them now, and she shows Elsbeth how to put a diaper on the baby."

Pretty Bean, the little unwed mother, had lost the baby she was expecting and was being cared for by the strange, mute Indian women who came from goodness-knows-where and disappeared after their work was done.

Ella hoped that she would soon emerge from her "trip."

Pretty Bean and Joe Quail

Silences were longer than periods of speech, but the lovers were in harmony of feeling, if not of thought. She lay propped up on cushions, her face more pinkly healthy than it had been for several months, and the Indian squatted beside her on his heels. It was an easy position for him which he could maintain for half a day, or, if need be, for all night. Four nights previously while Pretty had writhed in the screaming pain of premature birth, he had sat beside her in that position from dark until after sunrise, although a native midwife had officiated, first to swathe the girl's body in cold cloths, then, when prevention failed, to trickle pain-killing herb tea down her throat and to clasp her hands for the labor pulls. It was all over by the time Osta Eisen clattered the copper pots to start breakfast.

"You know what, Joe . . ."

"What?"

"I think it was because you didn't like him."

"How could I know if I liked him or not? He wasn't born yet."

"Just the same, I get presumptions sometimes, and I felt it when you—you know."

"Premonitions. And I hope you felt it!"

She giggled. "I mean I felt what was in your mind."

"You crazy or something? It was the shock of things being like they are, and the flight here, and this high altitude, and you washing clothes stooped over that way."

"Yeah. Maybe. But you didn't want him, did you?"

"I'd like it better to have my own kids caught in my trap. Plenty of time for that, though."

"You know what, Joe . . ."

"What?"

"I'd like for us to get married, like in church, you know."

"I know, but I don't see any churches around here."

"But there's a priest, even if Brother Smith don't come back."

"Okay, okay, we get married. But that will make me the boss, see?"

She giggled again and reached for one of his hands to lay against her cheek. "You'll work and make money for Bakie and June and me?"

"If I make the money, I'll do all the buying, see?"

"Uh-huh, that'll be nice. But you know what?"

"What?"

"I want you always to get trading stamps. I get such nice things for the babies with them."

Faintly, the sound of Hamilton's howl of protest was heard.

Joe blew his nose thoughtfully. "Not right to keep him penned up like an animal."

"What can you do? You said it isn't any ordinary lock on the door, but some kind of electric thing."

"Yuh." He rose, yawned widely and stretched, cat-like. "Think I take a walk around. Talk to High-Pockets, maybe."

"Why do you call him that? Shurtna don't have any pockets in that funny bathrobe thing he wears."

"Like we all have to wear. But Shur-Et-Na's got a pocket—in his sleeve, where he keeps his *kay.*"

Nadine

Nadine was on her third hunger strike. The first time was to protest the jailing of Roy Hamilton. That had come to an end when Garner had called on her to bring her a delicacy which he said his half-mother had prepared specially for her. She was going to remain stoical, but whoever heard of a "half-mother?" She laughed, and he laughed with her. Soon they were— She had known that would happen ever since she felt the magnetism of his eyes when they met hers at the entrance to the Pan-U building.

After that, she felt like eating.

Her second rebellion was against working in the fields with the men. Shurtna said *verna* shoots must be cut before the hot spring sun brought them to flower. She didn't understand why it was called *verna.* Plain old asparagus was all it was. She had never liked the stuff, anyway, and they'd had it at every meal for days. The morning that she had found it scrambled in some strong-smelling eggs she announced her hunger strike. That one had ended when she fainted from weakness and an Indian woman had force-fed her some snake-lizard broth, or something equally revolting. She decided to eat on her own to prevent that from happening again.

This time it was much more serious, however. In the two months they'd been marooned on the isolated Utah ranch she had not been allowed to have any of her cosmetic aids. Mercifully, no mirrors had been provided, either, but when she caught sight of herself in the smooth surface of a pool she had almost flipped. The horrid old crone who stared back at her couldn't be herself! The face was raddled with a thousand wrinkles, muscles of the neck sagged, and what was the unforgivable worst was the two-inch gray part in her once beautifully chestnut hair. That, she decided, must be remedied at once. There was a bottle of hair color in her cosmetic case. She sent for Shurtna.

"There is absolutely no reason why our belongings should be kept from us," she argued.

The tall man, who was almost as attractive as his son, smiled blandly.

"One of the things we are learning in this unfortunate time is how to do without almost everything we thought we needed."

"Aren't we the nice old schoolmaster!" she mocked. "A little lesson in Robinson Crusoe living—or was it Rip Van Winkle?"

"A little of both, I think you'll find."

"Joke—laugh, as the board says that's held up before a TV audience. Well, take your jokes and get out High Pockets. I'm going to sit here and contemplate my pretty little navel until I get my cosmetic case."

"Let me urge you to think carefully, my dear Nadine, because this time we will not resort to force-feeding. A first attempt at suicide can be an impulsive act which would have been reconsidered, but a second attempt is indicative of a deep death wish, which we respect." He withdrew.

Hugh Shipsted

Childhood had been a lonely time for Hugh, but the pain of aloneness became acute when Mother left for a few hours or a day. Once when he was five she had been gone a week attending a Grange convention in Milwaukee with his father. She wouldn't have returned then had he not become so ill that one of his uncles had telephoned her. Ever since that time he had gotten a sore throat when she was away for more than a few shopping hours.

When Tana had been gone for twenty-four hours, he had developed the same kind of raspy throat with chills, fever, and aches all over. The foul-tasting herb brews which Osta Eisen had forced upon him only made his condition worse. His chest pained so badly he was sure he was developing pneumonia, and his fever shot up dangerously.

The overseer, Shurtna, had brought a little old German lady to nurse him. She bathed him for fever, tucked hot stones around him when he chilled, but the congestion in his lungs refused to break up. He became delirious and got Mon and Tana mixed up in his dreams. There were consultations over him with both Shurtna and the German woman waving their bright wands around. Nothing helped.

On the fourth morning of his serious illness Tana came in like a flooding sunrise. His fever ebbed as he took her hand and pressed it to his lips, and by noon he asked for solid food.

She explained that she had to go to her family for a few days, that the messenger had come at night, and that she'd had to leave immediately.

"You could have left me a note, my darling. Or better yet, taken me with you. It's only fitting and proper that I should meet your family before the wedding."

"All will be handled properly, my beloved. Now you must sleep. We will talk when you are stronger."

She kissed his sleep-closed eyelids, then brushed her lips across his. "May you never fully awaken, my dear, helpless *gur*-cub!"

Alexander Curry

There were many unanswered questions in Curry's mind, but he was not sure he wanted answers to them. It made his flesh crawl when he speculated on what *could* be. Again and again he went over the details of the abduction—there was no question but that's what it had been—and again and again he went over events that had transpired at the "ranch." He fervently wanted to believe they were in Utah. It was expedient to adhere to the original fiction for the sake of those who might panic if the illusion were broken. Also, he wanted to counteract the unkind and obviously false propaganda that Hamilton perpetrated. Most certainly, they were not prisoners of war. For one thing, they had been treated too well.

However, he realized that they were under some kind of influence, or, as his Iowa grandmother would have said, a "spell." There was the weird music at night, the chirping voices that receded like scampering rats when one came fully awake, and also the unexplained wand-waving, communication without words, and mysterious goings and comings.

For instance, he knew he had not been asleep the night before when he heard the scream of a human frightened and in pain. He had heard scurrying feet and had gotten up to look out but had found that his door was locked down. (Why should doors of a guest cabin operate like garage doors?) There were voices, but he hadn't been able to make out words—were they speaking English? Then Osta Eisen's foghorn came on.

"It was dogs I was going to catch for a coat collar, not people in the pantry!"

There was more mumbling, then Osta again. "If they don't work in the fields, it's good enough they should go hungry."

Shurtna explained. "You see, Osta-Na, we can't let them come together, not yet. And our people are much better suited to field work . . ." Mumbling, then, "That's where I think he's wrong, but results will show."

Who were these mysterious people for whom food must be stolen at night?

His reverie was interrupted by a loud and insistent clatter at the oven. Osta was banging copper pots together and shouting.

"Help! Come quick, everybody!"

Brock Gunnison, who was working in a nearby field, dropped his hoe and ran. Following him, Curry remarked on the fact that Joe Quail was absent. The Indian had been with them at first, but had evidently slipped away unnoticed during the morning rest period. Also, Gar-Na had taken that occasion to go on what Ben-Ad called a "woman hunt." The engineer had been occupied repairing a piece of farming equipment.

"Look!" Osta threw out her arms in an operatic gesture.

The earthquake of that morning had been unusually severe, and hot flakes of pumice still sifted down. Curry expected no less than a fissure in the earth, or a volcano rising like a *verna* shoot from the plateau.

Wide Lens

Nadine thrust her head out of her cabin. She was gaunt and hollow-eyed, but still holding to her hunger strike. "What're you trying to do, Eisen, wake up the dead?"

"Ach! Dumb clucks!" Osta spat. Then she softened in accordance with the new image she was trying to create. "I mean, don't you got eyes in your heads? He's *gone!*"

Ben-Ad came up with Gar-Na, who looked a little rumpled from the love tryst in which he had been surprised. The engineer twirled the rod in his hand, and the younger man fumbled in his sleeve for his. His hand came away empty.

"My *kay*—it's gone!" he said aloud.

Ben-Ad pointed to the restraint hut where Hamilton had been imprisoned. It was at the end of the slave quarters. The door was pushed up full against the high lintel and the hut was, of course, empty.

Pretty Bean scrambled out of her sick bed. Bakie crept out beside her when she pushed the door up. He was captured by Elsbeth, who stilled his wails of frustration with a rag doll.

"What's all the racket about?" Pretty asked. "He's been right here with me." She eyed her offspring without indicating a desire to coax him back to her side.

"Not your snot-nosed— Not Bakie," Osta explained. "Laosy-mouthed Hamilton, that's who."

Ben-Ad asked, "How long?"

"Just now," Osta panted. "I take some slops to the *tana* pool, and when I come back his door was up. It wasn't that way when I went down the hill."

"He's probably hiding in the shrubbery by the river," Gar-Na guessed. He was ill at ease without his *kay,* but apparently determined to make up for having shirked his duty in the field. "Unless someone gave him clothing, he can't go far, especially without footwear."

"The question is," Ben-Ad pressed, "who let him out. It could have been only someone with a *kay.*"

They turned questioning glances on Id-Mar-Ok as she emerged from Hugh Shipsted's cabin. She negated their suspicion with a wave of her *kay,* then added aloud, "It couldn't have been Shur-Et-Na, either. He left some time ago to confer with Bov-No-Urr in the next Project. Gerda wouldn't think of doing such a thing; besides, I doubt if she could lift the door with her *kay.*"

"Were there any strangers around?" Ben-Ad asked of Osta.

"Only the girlfriend of Gar-Na from down the river, but she waited over in his cabin till he came from the field. Joe Quail came in early from the field for a drink of my home-made berry juice. He said he's got a cramp in his stomach. I told him, 'More sick people we don't need,' and he said he'd be the nurse for Pretty Bean for a while."

Id-Mar-Ok looked in the girl's cabin and gestured that Quail wasn't there.

"He went to my mother's and brought back the children," Osta volunteered.

Ben-Ad shouted, "Quail! Joe QUAIL!" When there was no answer, he whirled on Gar-Na and asked a silent question.

The young man gestured hopelessly. "I just don't know. I may have dropped it somewhere."

"You wouldn't need it for what you were doing," the engineer observed acidly.

Brock Gunnison, who had been testing his ulcer with some of Osta's berry juice, spoke. "If you mean those rod things, I think maybe Joe knows how to use one. I've seen him practicing sleight-of-hand tricks with one."

"That thorn-points it," Ben-Ad summed up. "Joe Quail can use a *kay* and got hold of one to open the door for Hamilton."

Hugh Shipsted, who had tottered to his door to listen, laughed weakly. "What's so strange about that? Anybody can use a key if he has one."

Ben-Ad, at the cracking point, whirled on him. He had never liked the farmer, and liked him less since Id-Mar-Ok appeared to be taking his suckling-*gur* glances seriously.

Before he could speak, a pottery mug smashed into the door frame beside Hugh. Brock had thrown it.

Ben-Ad thanked him silently as Hugh retreated. The engineer turned to Gar-Na. "Take Brock and Curry back to the field. I'll get some *criven* from Bov-No-Urr and start the search."

Gar-Na took his *kay* and spoke silently.

The engineer gasped. "The *dzos!* And Quail with a *kay!* They might just get one off the ground!" He caught the rod that Gar-Na threw and left on the run.

Brock cast an inquiring glance at Nadine's cabin. "I'm afraid there's something wrong. Her door—"

Gar-Na spun him around and headed him toward the field. "So she has pulled down her door to close out the smell of cooking. The old girl must be desperately hungry by now."

Brock still hung back. "I think we should see . . ."

"She's being cared for," Curry reassured him. "Shurtna won't let anyone in his care come to harm."

The men had barely reached the edge of the field when the earth moaned deeply and broke into a series of crackling explosions. Gar-Na rolled into the trench where bundles of harvested *verna* shoots had been deposited, and the others followed. In the courtyard Osta dived under the massive center table, pulling the two children after her. Osta clung to Elsbeth, Elsbeth to Bakie, and Bakie to the rag doll. Pottery clattered to the ground, and copper utensils danced like living things on the tossing waves of ground. Wild dogs yelped and streaked for the deeper jungle, and the *gurs* huddled together in a whimpering heap.

The Diary

The earthquake completed our courtship. I was leaning over Hugh's pallet to draw the blankets around him when the buckling earth pitched me down beside him. We clung together at first in fright, then with growing awareness of each other. Before long our bodies were straining in desire, and he led me, tenderly and gently, through the ritual of union.

"Darling Tana," Hugh whispered when the tumult without and within had quieted, "we must be married at once."

I touched my lips to his. "At once," I promised with love welling up within me like a warm geyser.

Lifting my kay *I stroked it gently across my own forehead, then across that of my first lover.*

"I, Id-Mar-Ok of the Precious Blood Clan of Ok-Nokken, take thee, Hugh Shipsted of Black Earth, Wisconsin, twentieth century, for mate of bridal bower and work yoke, of ceremony and sorrow, for father of my children, for master of my household, for Sun and guiding star of my life."

Hugh smiled up at me from the depths of his hypnotic dream. "Always seem to find myself in a tunnel."

A chill seized me. Skin bumps rose prickly all over my body, and a trembling possessed me. I tucked hands into my sleeves and bit my lower lip to keep my teeth from chattering. Had Hugh's disease penetrated my physical immunities? I knew it had not; my chill was no more disease of body than his had been. It was caused by a cold shaft of reality penetrating my emotional core. Perhaps it was a glimpse down the "tunnel" of which he had spoken. I saw the time when wife and nurse would split apart. The nurse would be needed always, but as wife I would find myself orbiting around a sun with warmth but no radiance of light, alone in the dreamy blackness of life without mind. When my thoughts soared, as was the nature of my mind, they would soar alone.

I had to think. Unsteadily I groped for the door, trying to hold myself upright on limbs as weak as verna *stalks.*

"Darling," Hugh called, his voice oozy with love and sleep, "you will be with me always, won't you?"

I did not answer or look back.

Wide Lens

"Grossmutter!"

The little girl's terrified shriek brought Osta rushing into the courtyard.

"What is it, dear?"

"He—there!" She made a sweeping gesture. "He is choking her," she sobbed. "A naked man, holding her down, choking her!"

Id-Mar-Ok, stepping out of Hugh's cabin, asked in alarm, "Where? Who?"

"Her!" This time Elsbeth's pointing was more definite. "Nadine—er, Miss Wherry."

Osta and the young woman exchanged glances of understanding.

"Never mind," Osta soothed. "Nadine won't let herself get hurt. I think maybe she has ended her hunger strike and will want something to eat. Help me pick up the pots now so we can make her some soup."

"Yes, Grandmother."

While the older woman and the little girl collected the scattered utensils and swept away the shards of broken pottery, Id-Mar-Ok raised her *kay* to inform her co-workers that Nadine was ending her hunger strike and that Roy Hamilton had been found.

Nadine had not finished her second bowl of soup when Brother Smith sauntered into the courtyard and seated himself beside her.

"Any more where that came from? They don't feed a person in that place, and I didn't like it, anyway, so when the Lord opened the door with the earthquake I just came back."

He still wore the peaked cap of the mindless who were confined for special care. Again Id-Mar-Ok raised her *kay,* this time in a more urgent summons. Shur-Et-Na arrived almost at once.

Smith caught his robe. "The animals need me, Bolly. You've got to let me stay. I heard them whimpering clear down there, so when the Lord let me out, I crawled on my hands and knees to get to them, and they just climbed all over me. See—" He indicated his muddied robe. "I've got their paw-prints on me."

Shur-Et-Na stared at him in pity and indecision. Smith still clutched his robe.

"Don't send me back to that place, Bolly. I don't want to be locked up again with that crazy old man. He talked about Hitler all the time, then he'd say 'Eeeee.' It could affect a person's mind being around somebody like that."

The Project Leader communicated silently with his assistant. She nodded somberly.

"We must decide—many things."

Chapter XV

Alexander Curry

Field work had strengthened long unused muscles considerably, but there was a limit to Curry's endurance. He had been forced to rest a moment. The men, including the dour priest and the unwilling Hamilton, had been pressed into the work of cutting cane stalks—or the cane-like plant that provided sugar for the "ranch," as Curry insisted everyone call it. The summer sun was warm, though blurred to a purplish tint by smoke and ashes from the constantly belching volcanoes. Flying insects, which included some bird-sized moths with crazy-quilt wings, flitted around the bales of *glig* stalks. Curry had resolved not to use the Indian—or Hawaiian—words for items, but some things, including this peculiar cane, had no English equivalent. As a matter of fact, he had tried to avoid thought of any kind because it led to speculation, and speculation about the "ranch" and the strange natives, about the peculiar plant and animal life, about the earthquakes and the volcanoes . . . Perhaps the violent nuclear explosions had brought them forth from plateaus or even cornfields, as had been the case of Paracutín in Mexico. He longed for someone with whom he could talk, and again considered trying to break through barriers the sullen priest had thrown up around himself.

"I've been dying for somebody to talk to," Vera Simpson said breathily.

Curry moved over to allow her to sit beside him on the rock outcropping, but other than that he offered her no encouragement. The strident follower of Brother Smith's Everlasting Light was by no means the answer to his wish. He said nothing, but couldn't bring himself to be rude.

She hitched nearer to him and panted into his ear. "Maybe you can make that wooden Indian listen to reason. I've tried, goodness knows I've tried, but he just twirls his little rod and walks away. By rights, it should be Brother Smith's place, but he's sort of resigned his authority to the Indian—Bolly or Shurtna, whatever his name is. And sometimes I don't believe he's even a Christian—a lot of the Indians were never converted, you know. I'm sure that includes Joe Quail. Don't you think so?"

"Perhaps," Curry said cautiously. He had been watching Brock Gunnison, whose sunbrowned shoulders rippled smoothly in the cane-cutting rhythm. No doubt all of them had benefitted from the close-to-nature living, but on Brock it showed the most.

"I'm glad you agree with me about Quail," Vera persisted, "because what I have to say concerns him."

"You must excuse me." Curry beamed a professional smile her way and rose.

She laid hold of one of his arms. "You've got to listen. You're the only one who can help."

"Yes." He freed himself but did not move away.

"You see—" Her idea of a whisper was something that could be heard for no more than a hundred yards. "There's foul fornication going on all around us. There, I've said it. What've you got to say to that?"

Curry chose words carefully. "Perhaps some of our associates don't have the high moral standards you and I have."

"High moral standards! They don't have *any!* That Nadine Wherry, as she wants to be called—a married woman with no regard for her marriage vows, let alone reverence! She started out on a rendezvous with Brock Gunnison—and I've found out that he's married, too—then switched to Garner, and he was through with her quick enough. Now she's living openly and brazenly with that foul-mouthed Laosy Hamilton."

"At any rate," Curry temporized, "she has persuaded him to cover his nakedness and to cease haranguing us about escape."

"He keeps talking to her about it, though. I can hear them, right through the door that they sometimes leave open a crack—all about a 'sweet little deal' that will buy her black lace panties. Black lace panties! Now I ask you, would any God-fearing woman consider wearing such things, let alone accepting them from a— Well, I just don't use the words that describe what I think of him."

"I'm afraid that nothing will reform either Hamilton or Nadine, and we're stuck here with them for the time being. Perhaps it would be best to just ignore them."

"I'm willing to give them a wide berth. After all, they're adults. But there's that little teen-age thing and Joe Quail. Good thing she lost that third illegitimate baby, if you ask me. But she'll get that way again, if she hasn't already, carrying on the way she is with that black Indian! There's just no one a decent woman can associate with!"

"Ella Pozniak seems a decent enough sort. Then there's the hostess . . ."

"Humph!" Vera sniffed. "Hadn't meant to mention her, since she's one of *Them,* but I'm not satisfied that her attentions to Hugh Shipsted are all they ought to be. I think he's a good man and a Christian, but you know how men are around temptation."

Curry smiled sadly and perhaps reminiscently.

"I can see you're very troubled, Vera—if you don't mind my calling you that—but what is there you think I could do?"

"Talk to that wooden Indian, for one thing. Get him to separate the non-married couples and to lock all the doors at night. Another thing, I think we ought to say grace at the table and have some good old-fashioned prayer meetings. Maybe a few souls can be rescued out of this carnal swamp, like little Elsbeth, and maybe Ella . . ."

"Wonderful idea, my dear Vera!" Curry applauded. "I'm sure you can get something of the kind going, gradually at first, maybe. Now I must join the others. We must each do his share, you know, as Shurtna has reminded us."

He escaped.

Osta Eisen

Trotting back from the storage cave where she had racked bundles of *glig* stalks, Osta encountered her mother with the baby, Junie, in her arms. The two women exchanged a few sentences in German, the older woman pointing with her free hand. Osta then ran back into the cave to emerge a moment later balancing two stacks of empty baskets.

"Grab a basket, everybody!" she called out in her fire-gong voice. "My mother says groundberries are ripe in the woods. We must hurry and get them before the *ginga* birds eat them up."

After a silent exchange with flashing *kays* between Gar-Na and his "half-mother," he let the men go with the women. It gave him an opportunity to run to his demanding bride. At the river, Ella and Pretty Bean dropped the ropes of clothing they had wrung out of the cold water, and in the courtyard Nadine threw aside the doll whose face she had been painting. Elsbeth, eagerly awaiting the outcome, snatched up the wet-faced doll, took the hand of her charge, Bakie, and ran after the women. Only the priest remained behind.

Osta bulldozed her way through underbrush and pushed aside streamers of prickly moss that festooned the tree branches. Gerda, forgetting they were not in a gentle German wood, trustingly followed her daughter. The baby in her arms cried out several times as moss scratched her face.

Wide Lens

An impenetrable tangle of vegetation had taken over the area where the river fanned out in the broadening valley, and leading away from this jungle were thickets of young fern, thorn bushes, and some lofty hardwoods swathed in trailing moss. The ground underneath was spongy with lichen. Long-necked birds, some with crests of brilliant plumage, flitted in the branches overhead. Bright-colored lizards of various sizes scampered over the ground, and tiny ape-like creatures that were mostly arms and tail screamed warnings to one another.

Brock Gunnison, walking beside Curry, indicated their surroundings with a wave of the cane-knife he had retained.

"Are you still hanging onto the Utah myth?"

Perplexity traced itself on the lecturer's face. "I'd no idea there was anything like this in Utah."

Brock gave up with a grunt of disgust.

Hamilton, following close behind them, let out a bellow when a thorny branch slapped back into his face.

"Crissake, if you don't know how to cut your way through a jungle with a machete, let a man do it!"

He reached for the knife, but Brock held onto it. "Why didn't you bring your own knife?"

"Garner took it away from me. Guess he was afraid I'd lead an escape out of this one-horse prison camp. They know I'm the only one that can do it."

Osta's froggy voice cut off their conversation.

"This food comes right out of the lap of Mother Nature," she lectured. "They don't have stuff like this in your supermarkets or in the chemically fertilized playpens they call farms nowadays . . ."

"Eeeee!" Ella screamed and pointed to a sluggish reptile that moved into her path to lasso a lizard with its long tongue.

Osta laughed. "You lived in Chicago with a million poison snakes, now you squeal over a harmless one!"

"He had a head like a pheasant," Ella sobbed.

"Don't you know a bird from a snake? If that's how dumb you are, it's time you got out into the country for a little education."

Then, catching sight of a vine runner on the ground with berries glistening on it like Christmas tree lights, she snatched it up and followed it into the shaded wood.

"Berries we've got now. Everybody get busy. You, too, Elsbeth, and Bakie help. He is not too young to learn about the food of Nature."

The laden vines covered the ground and entwined themselves in the hanging moss. There were enough berries to fill all the baskets, and soon everyone was busy stripping the reddish-purple globules from long vine runners. Before long the group had scattered.

Suddenly there was a roar in the jungle as though a tornado had struck, then Osta's frenzied scream, *"Meine Mutter! Meine Mutter!"*

Curry, who was closest to her, ran to the scene. Then halted in horror. A huge rhinoceros-like animal was mauling and tearing at the older woman who lay on the ground. The baby, Junie, was thrown from her arms and lay close to the animal's huge hind feet, squawling, but so far unharmed. Pretty Bean ran up and dived toward the child, but Curry pulled her back.

At that moment Ella ran in, and when the animal surged forward to horn the now unconscious Gerda, she snatched up the baby. She stumbled and would have been trampled had not Brock lunged at the animal's hindquarters to drive the machete like a spear into one of the leathery haunches. It remained there, quivering. The beast roared and changed course enough for him to pull Ella and the baby to safety. Pretty Bean took it from the near-fainting Ella, then she, herself, fainted in Curry's arms.

Osta, hysterical and out of her senses, tried to rescue the torn body of her mother, moving in almost under the pillar-like legs. Hamilton grappled with her. Everyone screamed. The beast paused, blinked reptilian eyes at the two in its path, then lowered its one-horned head to charge. Hamilton threw Osta clear; Quail caught her and with Brother Smith's help dragged her to safety behind a fern tree. The pilot stood like a foolishly brave matador before the charging animal, then, when its breath was upon him he dived and slid on the ground made slippery with blood and trampled berries. He went between the front legs, his clothes ripping on the horned toes that flew past him. He collided with Gerda's body, was unable to throw it clear and rolled to one side as the great hind feet slammed down like ten-ton pile drivers. Nadine darted in to pull him out of the beast's path. He tried to return, but she clung to him, throwing him to the blood-slippery ground, and falling on top of him.

Hugh Shipsted pulled them to their feet.

"Awfully dangerous to fool around the bulls in breeding season."

Brock, who had taken charge of Elsbeth and Bakie, emitted a bellow of rage that vied with that of the beast. "Knock it off, farmer, for Je-sus Christ's sake, knock it off!"

Vera Simpson, the only one of the group not involved in the action, stood to one side frozen in horror. She glanced at Brock angrily.

"You have taken the name of the Lord in vain!" Then she fainted.

The great animal continued to plunge back and forth in rhythmic orgiastic thrusts at the body, spraying it with bursts of sex emissions, urine, and excrement. Tree-things screamed, scolded, and swished away, only to return with larger numbers of their kind. A huge and torpid reptile, apparently attracted by the odor of death, wriggled into the path of the beast and added its own burst body to the befouled scene.

Curry called to members of the horror-frozen group. "We must go. There's nothing we can do for the dead woman, and it's too dangerous to stay here."

They went, he and Hamilton dragging the hysterical Osta between them. Shur-Et-Na came to meet them. Osta fell into his arms, and he wept with her. Vera tried to relate what had happened, but he silenced her with a wave of his *kay*.

"You're a mind-reader, that's what you are!" she accused.

"Mind-reading never hurt anyone," Nadine snapped. She supported the limping Hamilton.

The priest, apparently aware of some sort of excitement, thrust his head out of his cabin. With a sharp and frightened glance at Nadine he slammed the door down.

The startled Nadine asked, "What bit him?"

"Mind-reading, Baby," Hamilton said with a knowing wink at Quail.

Alexander Curry

There was nothing to be done at the "ranch." Everyone was in a state of shock, even the urbane Shurtna. Several silent Indian women bustled around the oven to prepare dinner. No one appeared for the meal. Curry picked up a peeled stick of *glig* to sustain him and walked off into the desert. He needed to think. Yet he tried not to think. He could not sort out the baffling things which he was sure had happened. His sensory impressions were too strong to have been delusions. He tried to shut out guesses, yet they beat against his mind like swarming bats in a cave.

He became tired after the climb away from the riverlands. He rested on a flat rock and watched an angry sun set behind the spitting volcanoes.

"Is this a private seat or may I share it with you?" A man panted up beside him.

Currry's flesh crawled, and he was almost afraid to turn. The voice was one he knew—from a long time ago.

"Alex!" the man exclaimed, pulling him around.

"Howard!"

The men regarded each other in shocked amazement, then both spoke at once.

"What are you doing in Utah?"

"What are you doing in China?"

"China?"

"Utah?"

McMillan and Curry were silent while anger cooled from the sunset. Volcanoes spat red jets against a dark gray curtain, and night insects darted through floating flakes of pumice.

"Something besides geography is screwed up." This from McMillan.

"Yes, Howard. You were in a 'brain drain,' weren't you? I read your name in the mini-paper the morning that—that morning."

"Sylvester Markham of Santa Cruz got the impression that we were being brought to China to help the Chincoms with some sort of social problem. We were brought out here to an oasis in the Gobi Desert. Our clothes were taken away, and we were quartered in funny little cabins where the doors open upward, like garage doors. They said we were going to have to do some kind of field work, but they've kept us building a bathhouse, over and over. They say earthquakes shake it down, but if that's true, the earthquakes have chisels or some kind of tools . . ."

"Who are 'They?' "

"I don't know. Some of them have kind of an Oriental look, but more like Malayans. The head man, Bovnurr, acts like a Dean of Students—talks a lot, says nothing. The rest of them are silent, do some kind of deaf-and-dumb talk with bright rods.

"For a while we speculated a lot about where we were and what was expected of us, then one of our number, Doctor Emory-Leonard—on sabbatical from Oxford, tense, brittle sort—went over the brink. They took him off to some sort of hospital, and we can sometimes hear him screeching—eerie. Since then, we haven't said much. We just build the bathhouse, and the women weave, and that sort of thing. Laura Lindholm's the only one that's holding up at all well, and she gets kind of shaky sometimes. But tell me, how are things in Utah?"

Curry shuddered. "It's not funny, Howard." He then related his story, taking it from the incident of the odd-looking hostess knocking the suicide pill from his hand and ending with the scene in the jungle.

A few of the brightest stars pricked through the curtain of smoke and ash, and as the patterns above them slowly changed, they asked each other questions and sought answers.

“We’re neither in Utah nor in China,” Dr. McMillan summed up, “but where *are* we?”

Curry shrugged. “Young planet of some kind—somewhere. The vegetation and animal life is—I don’t know the names of the ages of Earth—but I’d say they’re not long out of the slime. Yet the people are more advanced than we were: light without wires, music without instruments . . .”

“And mind-to-mind communication,” McMillan added. “But somehow I can’t believe we were transported through space. The trip wasn’t long enough, for one thing. All I remember was some kind of terrible blue light.”

“We went through it, too. The flare from nuclear explosions, I took it to be.”

“I’m not a physicist, but I’m sure it wasn’t that kind of light.”

“Maybe that was part of the hypnosis process. Our whole group, unless it is the German woman who claims our overseer as her father, has been kept under partial hypnosis. The Wisconsin farmer is still under, even after today’s shocking experience. What sent Brother Smith off his rocker was that his ‘goats’ had soft feet and necks that were too long.”

“I’ve seen those creatures—they pull sleds and give milk, and I think supply the wool our women weave. Look like the South American guanaco.”

“I never saw anything like them. Funny, at first they looked like goats to me, then after Smith cracked up, I saw them as small camels, sort of stupid things . . .”

“Guanacos are kind of small humpless camels.”

Curry sighed with relief. “I’m sure reality is getting through to both of us. Maybe your group, being scientists, can figure it out.”

McMillan shook his head in doubt. “I don’t dare tell the others. You see, Alex, the world of the academician today is a very small place, and horribly real.” He stirred the gritty dust with the toe of one boot. “For instance, Emory-Leonard’s universe was no bigger than the enclosed globe he claims Adolf Hitler believed in. A little too much reality made him just as batty as Hitler’s supposed to have been. Trouble is, Alex, the intellectual of today knows just about everything. There’s no room in his little mind for anything new. The superstitious man of old who believd in miracles had more flexibility."

Curry nodded. "The religious fanatic, too. Brother Smith says God decided to change his goats, but they're still his goats."

"I'm religious," McMillan reminded him. "Remember, that's what we didn't see eye-to-eye on?"

"It wasn't religion," Curry said. "It was the action of the churches—vast difference."

"Not important now. You see, while Brother Smith's God performs sleight-of-hand tricks, mine is big enough to oversee a Universe billions of light-years in diameter, with an infinite number of life forms swarming on a million-million planets, and time without beginning or end . . ."

"Time," Curry mused. "Of course, it's impossible!"

"Hmn, time. Once a long time ago, according to some scientists, there was a Doomsday on the world. Something pushed the Moon too close and the oceans went wild and destroyed everything on land. Do you suppose—?"

Curry rose and yawned widely. "We're not going to solve it, Howard, and we have to get a little sleep before you have to go back to building the bathhouse and I have to cut *glig*."

With mumbled good nights, they parted.

Chapter XVI

Gur-cream clotted in cereal bowls, and the white sticks of *glig* oxidized and curled, soon to spill unnoticed off the platter. None of the adults at the table was interested in breakfast. Osta had not appeared, nor had Elsbeth, and, as usual, the priest remained in his hut with the door raised only ankle-high. Curry tried to rack up the *glig* sticks, but could not bring order out of the little chaos. He absently chewed one and laid it aside unfinished. He wanted to tell of his experience of the night before, but feared the reactions, or, more correctly, feared there would be no reaction.

Bakie Bean finished his cereal and sat squirming on the bench trying to catch his mother's eye. She was spooning gruel into Junie's face without much regard for the location of the child's mouth.

Joe Quail toyed with a *kay*. Vera Simpson's head shot up like that of a startled fowl.

"You've got one of their rods, Joe Quail!"

He tossed it into the air and caught it. "Gives me something to do with my hands."

Pretty regarded him adoringly. "Take Bakie to pottie. The way he's wriggling around, it's just about too late."

The Indian snatched up the dripping boy and ran to their cabin with him.

Roy Hamilton lifted his face like a dog about to howl.

"Oh, gimme a girl, a sweet bay-bee gur-rl,
With hair of gold and a corkscrew cur-rl . . ."

Nadine shushed him. "Not now, Roy, it's too soon."

He quieted for a moment, then burst out: "What're we doing sitting around mourning one o' *Them?* Sure, I tried to get her away from that rhino—human being against a wild animal, you'll try to save the human. But that don't mean we owe *Them* anything. I've had enough of this Goddamn' ass-kissing. All of you pucker up every time one o' them gollywogs comes into sight." He made an unsightly *moue*. " 'Yes, Mister Shurtna'; 'I think so, Mister Bennett'; 'You first, Garner!' Christ, I've seen hundreds of Americans killed by *Them,* and we didn't even have time for mourning our own . . ."

Nadine kicked him as a group of *criven* crossed the courtyard bearing a covered stretcher the under part of which was stained the color of blood and crushed berries.

Brock rose. "Think I'll find out if we're going to work in the field today."

Hamilton made the ugly *moue* again. " 'Yes, Mister Shurtna.' "

Ella began to clear the table, and Nadine pulled Hamilton away.

"We're not selling anything here, Roy. Let's talk it over in private."

"Talk, is it? Times have changed." He winked insinuatingly at those still around the table.

Brother Smith went to his goats, and Hugh Shipsted wandered off in search of "Tana." Pretty Bean took the sleeping Junie to her cabin.

Ella caught sight of a plate on top of the oven. "Has anyone fed the priest?"

A tense silence followed. No one liked to be reminded of the strange sullen man who kept himself caged like an animal. Vera sighed as though resigning herself to an unpleasant task and began to pile food on the warm plate.

"Osta always feeds him, or the little girl."

Curry took the plate from her. "Let me. I need some busy work."

At that moment a whirlwind struck. It was Osta Eisen, arms waving, skirts billowing.

"Nein! Nein!" She snatched the plate from Curry. "Only mush he gets in the morning, *mit* sweetening and *gur*-cream. And only he takes from my hand or Elsbeth's."

Her face was blotched and puffed from weeping, her eyes swollen almost shut, and her breath came in involuntary sobs.

Elsbeth ran up to her. "Grandmother, it is no good to cry like this. You know, you tell me crying will not mend the broken dollie."

"I know, und it will not bring back to life my beautiful *Mutterchen!"* She drew her full skirt over her face and wept noisily into it.

Curry and Vera made feints of comfort, but she was unaware of them. Ella prepared a bowl of mush and handed to the little girl, who started toward the cabin of the recluse. Osta dashed after her and snatched away the bowl.

"You take now some food to Grandpa Shur. He must eat, too."

Ella prepared another bowl of mush, which Elsbeth carried off in the direction of Shur-Et-Na's quarters.

Osta shoved the bowl under the priest's door and wailed loudly. "Father, you must hear me! I have sinned; I have sinned terribly. I killed *meine* own mother. Pray wit' me, Father, please pray wit' me. I give anything for one small hope that I can be forgiven."

"Go away," the man inside the cabin mumbled.

"Don't send me away in sinful misery, Father."

"Blessings not for murderers. Go!"

Osta moaned and sobbed louder. "Oh, Father, all the time you knew! It was a terrible mistake with Wilbur Eisen, like wit' my mother. He was crazy for money, and I was just crazy, I guess, when I put the poison in the boughten flour . . ."

She was still pouring out garbled confessions when Shur-Et-Na came to lift her to her feet. He tilted her wet face up to his own, which was becoming wet.

"You have much to weep over, daughter mine. You failed Gerda as a daughter because you did not catch the butterfly she directed toward you; you failed your children as a mother because you did not try to understand their longing and little sorrows; you committed the greatest of all wrongs against your husband. What happened yesterday was an accident, an accident caused by your careless exuberance. You can continue as the thoughtless sinner you now are, or you can touch the ground with that falsely proud head and taste the humility of the soil."

Shur-Et-Na dropped his arms from her and stepped back. He did not touch his *kay,* but kept his eyes on his weeping daughter. She stood tensely for a moment, her shoulders shaking and breath coming in gasps.

Near the oven Vera Simpson sank to her knees and began to pray. Curry knelt beside her, and Ella wavered a moment, then made the sign of the cross.

Slowly, Osta lowered herself to her hands and knees and leaned forward to touch her lips to the ground.

The Diary

Out of deference to the grief-torn Osta, we planned a ceremonial of burial for the mangled remains of Gerda Mayer. While Ben-Ad directed some criven *at digging a trench in the burial grounds, I took others inside the temple to prepare our music room for the twentieth-century burial rites. Not only would our hangings and plaques offend those of Christian faith, but also The People would be outraged if we allowed barbaric rites to be conducted in the presence of our own sacred symbols. It was therefore necessary to remove them for temporary storage.*

The slaves, who were allowed in our temple only to clean it, were uncertain about what they should touch. Consequently, I found myself performing most of the labor, and before long my hands became grimy, my face besmudged and garments dust-laden. I was far from my immaculate and scented best when the stiffly formal Project Administrator, Bov-No-Urr, touched my shoulder with his kay. *I had not seen him since I had returned from my home visit.*

"There is a matter that demands discussion between us," he said, using our formal spech.

I gave the slaves instructions about storing several armloads of hangings and cords in the caves, then seated myself on a bench in front of the Administrator. He was a heavy man with a large, beard-blackened face, thick neck and hairy hands. I couldn't help noticing that his flabby jowls were pocked with scars of much beard removal and that his bristling eyebrows were thick as jungle growth. Hairiness was generally regarded by The People as an indication of uncouthness, or closeness to the animal-like primitive. I'm sure that Bov-No-Urr would not have gotten the position he held had he not belonged to a clan of great wealth. I repressed a shudder of revulsion and waited for him to speak.

He leaned toward me and stroked my forehead with his kay, *indicating that the conversation was to be of a personal and confidential nature.*

"It is the matter of your twentieth-century lover-man," he began with pompous formality. "Your Project Leader, or father-of-work, and I have discussed his recruits in great detail, and with the exception of the so-called priest and this farmer I am satisfied that all of them are capable of carrying the Flame to emerging mankind beyond the second Destruction."

"Even the stupid and obscene Hamilton?"

Had we been communicating by words I would not have asked the question, but the thought had flashed through my mind before I could erect the proper barrier.

"Even Hamilton," the Administrator nodded. "He showed considerable ingenuity and bravery at the scene of the unfortunate jungle accident yesterday. He is crude indeed, but the world into which he is going is even more so."

"If you're going to pass Hamilton, why not the priest?" my runaway mental process questioned. "He is even nearer the primitive than the Laotian pilot, and might be able to form a needed link between the colony and the beast-men around them."

Bov-No-Urr considered my opinion seriously. "You are no doubt right, my dear. I shall reverse my decision, which you may convey to Shur-Et-Na. The priest, as you call him, is not only physically strong, he is also courageous, or he could not have endured the solitude he has imposed upon himself. Besides—" His thoughts raced on beyond the communication he intended for me. "We will not have to care for another reject in our limited facilities here.

"However, this is all digression." He pulled himself up stiffly. "We must return to the matter I came to discuss. Your Project Leader has reported on Hugh Shipsted's inability to emerge from the hypnotic state. Do you think, dear Id-Mar-Ok, that it would be kind to send such a childlike person into a raw, tooth-gnashing time?"

"I do not propose to *send* him, my Project Administrator, I propose to *take* him."

"The matter of your going *ig-saki* has not been properly discussed. It is something which the Noble Conclave should decide."

"My father conveyed my decision to the Conclave. He accepted it; the other nobles must do so."

"Nevertheless, I'm sure that a reversal of your hasty decision would overjoy your distinguished father, as well as your uncles and brothers . . . Would you not like to make them proud of you? Would you not like to brighten the last days of those dear to you?"

His mental screening was not good, but I permitted him to continue.

"Would not an elaborate ceremony of marriage give them the happiness they deserve? A wealthy and highly placed man could provide such a ceremony—jewel-embroidered robes, rich gifts, pomp and pageantry in mirror-lined chambers, magic pictures, music and dancing and merriment to make the noble Clan of Ok-Nokken forget the on-coming horrors of flood and flame."

"The Clan of Ok-Nokken does not choose to forget," I pointed out. "Those of our Precious Blood must savor the sweet pain of sacrifice. To distract them in their ceremonials would be cruel and uncouth."

"Nonsense!" he sputtered. "Every human being, whether of Precious or animal blood, clings to life and wants the utmost in comfort and pleasure which he can obtain. It is of course regrettable that so many of noble birth must die in the coming calamity, and I can understand the reason for all this anodyne of religion. But it is completely mad to die by ritual if we don't have to do so. Come to me as my bride, Id-Mar-Ok, and we will commandeer a dzo, take your parents and closest of kin, and escape to a time when we can reign as deities."

The crawling revulsion this crude proposal evoked in me caused me to shiver. I could find no words to reply to such a gross insult, and the obtuse Bov-No-Urr mistook my silence for wavering consent.

"You must regard it squarely, Id-Mar-Ok; this unfortunate recruit, Shipsted, is a mental cripple, helpless as a newborn gur. Though he might satisfy a momentary sexual craving, he can offer you nothing but a life of spiritual bleakness. And as for the time to which you have been assigned—" H shuddered expressively, and pressed his flabby body against mine.

I drew away and spoke verbally for emphasis. "I am not going ig-saki out of mere whim or the desire to satisfy carnal urges; I want to bear children, but I do not necessarily long for the pains of childbirth. I am aware of the fact that I am taking on a lifetime of nursing and catering to a mind that cannot flower. I shall have to endure great loneliness; in that time to which we are going, I shall have to fight for existence. I shall have to be the protector of my family in a world of fangs and cultural darkness. I shall experience a thousand deaths, whereas if I remained in the halls of my clan I would meet but one.

"If I forgot my vows and forsook my family traditions of faith to find carnal pleasure in a time of easy living, I *would die many times a thousand deaths. The Great Plan of our deity does not call merely for the preservation of human flesh, but for the preservation of the Flame, the spirit of worship, the love of beauty, the striving upward—the reach toward perfection. Unless I can be part of that Great Plan, I would prefer the most painful and lingering death."*

The response of my rejected suitor was lost in a blood-chilling cry that penetrated the temple walls. There were sounds of crashing doors and running feet, and we both hurried out to learn what had taken place.

Chapter XVII

Group Two

Dr. Howard McMillan was a competent lecturer. Even though institutions of higher learning no longer demanded the physical presence of lecturers in the classroom, he preferred to make frequent personal appearances before his students. He now put his abilities and experience to the test, speaking with sufficient detachment to appeal to the trained scientific mind, weaving in phrases colorful enough to catch the attention, and allowing emotion to creep into his voice in order to maintain human contact. Simply and briefly, he told his associates of his meeting with Alexander Curry, and of what Curry had told him.

He had already informed Laura Lindholm, who now shared his cabin, and as he spoke she affirmed his statements with an occasional nod of her head or an understanding smile.

Even the smug Dr. Markham found his convictions wavering. After a few sputters of "Oh, come now, Dr. McMillan," and "Surely you don't expect us to believe that," he subsided to a listening attitude.

This infuriated the fiery Dr. Vaughn Wright more than McMillan's tale did. He frankly and rudely refused to believe the speaker and wanted no one else to do so.

Irma Boyd withdrew slightly from him, but remained skeptical of what McMillan was relating.

Dr. Phillope Applebaum, who had found Vaughn Wright an interesting sex partner, was his partisan, although not his ideological convert. She had no beliefs other than hedonistic ones. While McMillan spoke, she had been engrossed in shaping and polishing her fingernails with a piece of pumice. Wright tried to involve her in heckling the speaker, but she merely smiled and lifted a foot to the bench on which she sat and began to work on her toenails.

"Stop that!" Wright batted the pumice out of her hand and slapped her.

McMillan, who had reached the point of Gerda Mayer's death in the jungle, paused to wait for order.

Markham shook his head at Wright. "This is a most interesting lecture. We don't have to believe it, but it provides a little variety in our otherwise dull existence. Let's hear McMillan out."

"He's lying!" Wright shouted. "We're in the Gobi Desert! We're the guests of the Chin-coms! We're here to help them!" His face was livid and his eyes glazed with fury.

"Very well," Markham soothed, "that's your belief." He turned to the speaker and indicated he was to continue.

McMillan did so. "Suddenly an animal—Curry described it as a sort of reptilian rhinoceros, huge and less sophisticated than our mammals, as I believe our scientists would say . . ."

"Our scientists don't tell fairy stories!" Wright was on his feet, waving his arms. "We're not near any other settlement! We're not on the edge of any Cenozoic swamp! You're lying, that's what you are—just plain out-and-out malicious lying!"

He lunged at McMillan, but Markham tried to restrain him. The middle-aged man was no match for the young zealot. Irma Boyd rushed in to help Markham. Wright threw off both of them and dived at a pile of tools which the men had used to build the bathhouse.

"Vaughn!" Phillope Applebaum scolded. "That's carrying an argument too far!"

He paid no heed to her, seized a short-handled adze, and lunged at McMillan. Markham again grappled with him, but Wright tore away. With the force of his mad rage he chopped the blade at Markham. It went deep into his skull. The sociologist's eyes were open when he fell; he twitched once, then lay still. An enormous amount of blood gushed out in two or three spurts, but stopped when the heart ceased pumping.

Wright, now completely berserk, yelling in mad gasps, scarcely noticed the body of his victim. He pulled another tool from the pile, this time a heavy crowbar, and flayed about without aim. Irma Boyd fell with a deep gash in her right side. Phillope leaned down to help her and caught the crowbar in the side of the head. It mashed in her skull, and she did not move after she fell.

McMillan threw Laura Lindholm out of the danger arc and managed to time his movements so that he could drag the injured Irma Boyd to safety. Y-Stan-Urr and the mute *dzo* pilot ran up, but before they could raise *kays* to control the crazed man, the pilot was recapitated by the wildly swinging crowbar. The Administrator's daughter fled, screaming for help.

Wright, barking in a high falsetto and carrying the crowbar in one hand and a sharp-edged trowel in the other, pursued her in kangaroo leaps. The girl reached the temple barely a man-length ahead of him. She jumped inside, and the attendant slammed the door down almost in the face of the crazed man. Wright changed direction and the pitch of his voice and bounded off toward the jungle.

Ben-Ad, who had heard the commotion, ran into the temple through the back entrance, his slaves, armed with digging tools, following closely behind.

"Let us hope," he commented after sorting out the facts from the hysterical Y-Stan-Urr's account, "that both Wright and the *zig-tag* vanquish each other."

The Project Administrator reproved him with a glare. "This is much too serious a matter to be dealt with frivolously. First, we must try to aid the injured recruit; second, get our recruits and personnel to a place of safety; and third, consider future steps to be taken."

Id-Mar-Ok and Ben-Ad, guarded by only two slaves with spades and their own *kays,* were dispatched to their own project to inform Shur-Et-Na of the situation. Bov-No-Urr, his daughter, and four slaves armed with more formidable digging tools set out for their courtyard. Nothing was seen of the crazed man, although considerable flutter and ape-chitter came from the jungle.

Combined Groups

The recruits were to dispatched at once. Bov-No-Urr and his terrified daughter reached Shur-Et-Na's project soon after Howard McMillan and Laura Lindholm arrived. The two fleeing recruits had tried to bring the injured Irma Boyd with them, but she had expired on the way. Fearing the return of the crazed Dr. Wright, they had abandoned the body. The Administrator and his daughter came upon it and directed slaves to take it and the others from the courtyard to prepare them for burial.

McMillan and Dr. Lindholm were near collapse from fright and shock. Their account of the mass murders greatly disturbed Shur-Et-Na's recruits, especially since they had not recovered from the horror of the jungle. Both Ella Pozniak and Vera Simpson showed signs of hysteria and had to be tranquillized by Id-Mar-Ok. Even Brother Smith and Hugh Shipsted were aware that something was badly amiss, and the priest raised his door to listen.

Roy Hamilton was quick to react. "High Pockets has got to get us out of this screwy Malaysian jungle *muy pronto,* or we get ourselves out. The Geneva Accord has got something to say about how prisoners of war are to be treated, and we can make demands."

"I'm with you, whatever you do!" Joc Quail was quick to offer.

"Me, too," Brock said. "Things have gone far enough. Time we got out of here."

Laura Lindholm, unable to follow the dialogue of the strange recruits, lapsed into cataleptic shock and sat rigid as a deactivized robot. McMillan tried to rouse her and when he could not, he put his head on folded arms and wept.

"We need some kind of help," he cried.

Id-Mar-Ok, who had returned from taking the two women to their cabin, touched him with her *kay*. "The Project Leaders are now considering your welfare, Dr. McMillan, and they will be here soon. Meanwhile, may I suggest a silent prayer, each to his own God."

"That's not good enough!" Hamilton roared, leaping to his feet.

The young woman directed a charge from her *kay* at him. "We have nothing stronger on hand, Mister Hamilton." She turned to Dr. Lindholm.

Hamilton sat down with a thump and let his drowsy head fall into Nadine's lap.

Curry and McMillan prayed. Brother Smith stared at them.

Pretty Bean, who had been cooing softly to the child in her arms, announced, "It's time for Junie's nap."

Hugh Shipsted yawned. "We could all use a little rest. Too much excitement recently." He turned to his "Tana," who was helping Laura Lindholm to a cabin. "Unless you have something for me to do, dearest, I think I'll lie down for a while."

"My goats are getting lonesome." Brother Smith started toward the animal shelter.

Shur-Et-Na, followed by the still-quaking Bov-No-Urr, appeared. Both raised *kays*, and those moving away from the table in the center of the courtyard halted. Shur-Et-Na spoke.

"We have an announcement which we are sure all of you will welcome. Tomorrow morning you will leave for your destined homes. Your belongings will be restored to you; there will be sleep-instruction tonight to prepare you for what lies ahead. Meanwhile, you will be in no danger. Men competent to deal with any contingency will remain on guard throughout the night, and in the morning you will be taken by *gur*-sled to the place for boarding the craft. I urge all of you to rest for a short time now, partake of a good meal which will be prepared for you, then retire early."

The Administrator, who had solemnly nodded agreement with each of Shur-Et-Na's sentences, spoke to McMillan.

"You and Dr. Lindholm will be made comfortable here and taken with this group to the destination we had in mind for you. There, you will embark upon the sociological work for which you received subconscious conditioning here at Naz-Co." He beamed his self-satisfied smile around the bewildered and partly hypnotized group. "Let me say to all of you on behalf of the Naz-Co Projects that never before have we sent graduates of our training courses on a more important mission, and never have we had greater confidence in the high ideals and the stout moral fiber of our trainees. You go with my blessing and in the care of our great God, Oom."

No one was quite sure what he was talking about, or what he said. While they were exchanging questioning glances, Bakie Bean ran to his mother and hid his face in her robe.

"Mommy, I have to go pottie, long time ago."

Chapter XVIII

Shur-Et-Na found his daughter in the quarters she had shared with her mother. She was busily tying bundles of clothing and directing Elsbeth in tying others. She didn't stop her work or slow the furious speed with which she assembled material for the packs.

"I got your message, my *Vater,* and I don't like it one stinking bit. Already I can get things out of your mind like you thought I couldn't, and I know that you are not keeping your promise of a decent burial service for *Mutter.* That animal won't come out of his hiding place, and by now already he has found that murderer and stomped him to death. There is no reason—"

Shur-Et-Na lifted his *kay* to halt her swift flow of words. "It's the man we take precautions against, Osta-Na. We have no way of knowing if the *zig-tag* has even seen him. For many years your mother and the women of the Project have gathered groundberries at the edge of the jungle, and this is the first time the beast has attacked. Our recruits can't stand any more shock, even if they weren't in some danger. Besides, there's no need to keep them here longer. They're as ready as they ever will be for release . . ."

Osta waved an imperious hand. *"Ja, ja,* we go back no fifty t'ousand years and leave you here like you were with three other wives and a lot of children you don't even bring around and introduce to me. Elsbeth—" She turned to the girl. "Get now that smoked leg of *gur* and the sack of cured *glig* sticks to tie up in blankets. And we need some more of the nice cord we got from the cave by those dusty draperies."

"Cord? Draperies?" the project leader repeated. "Osta-Na, my dear . . . Stop!" he ordered the little girl who was outside the door. "Those cords are part of the sacred hangings from the temple! They can't be profaned! Besides, you can't take food of any kind through the Blue Belt. It would crumble to dust."

Osta sat heavily on a bundle. "All I know is what I get from your under-conscious, my father. And like your under-wash, maybe you don't change it often enough. I know I am going fifty t'ousand years—"

"Much more than that, my dear daughter." The Project Leader seated himself on another bundle, making sure he did not touch the cord.

Elsbeth stood respectfully to one side, but was growing restless. "May I go find Bakie now? He's lonesome for me. I heard him crying."

"We're in mourning, and out of this house you don't go for play."

"But, *Grossmutter*—"

"Sit down, my dear great-granddaughter." Shur-Et-Na motioned to a cushion, and when the girl was seated and had turned her large, thoughtful eyes to him, he went on: "Tomorrow, Elsbeth, you're going to have to be a grown woman. You will be in a world very different from this, and very different from your home . . ."

"Why, Great-grandfather?"

"Because it is a part of the Plan which we must follow. Your own world in which your mother and father, aunt and cousins lived was destroyed by terrible explosions. You were brought here with your grandmother and some other people to learn how to care for yourselves and how to teach the people of the new world to become civilized. At first it will take all your strength and all your knowledge just to live, to make some kind of shelter for yourselves and to find food. It is not possible to take much from here except what you carry in your heads and what you wear. Do you understand, dear girl, why you must be grown up tomorrow?"

"Yes, Grandpa Shur. Now may I go to say goodbye to my dollie?" She embraced him and ran out the door.

Osta and Shur-Et-Na sat quietly, their eyes on each other. They communicated without words, she drawing wisdom and serenity from him, he taking strength and courage from her. An earthquake rocked them and threatened to spill the cabin roof down upon them, but neither moved or spoke aloud. The earth had settled and the dusk had deepened to dark when they embraced and parted.

The Diary

The night was starlit and still; the angry red moon had not yet made its appearance, and the earth rested after a series of shocks that had threatened the small, sturdy dimds. *Several were cracked, and ash lay thick on the ground. Music, diffused and softened to the subliminal point, told plaintively of the hopes and the heartbreaks of The People who had brought order and beauty and spiritual love to the planet. Although the partially hypnotized recruits seldom heard it, they nevertheless absorbed it into their psyches.*

I savored every morsel of that night, which was to be the last in my home world. I memorized the cry of the ginga-*bird, the small cries of the* gings, *the sighs of the fronds of fern as they brushed gently against each other, and the rustle of leaves which were beginning to fall. The Naz river gurgled playfully over dams caused by rockslides, sending up a spray of sweet-scented mist.*

The nearby jungle stirred ominously, sometimes giving forth a shriek of death, but nothing had been seen of the madman since he entered it. The recruits, including the sensitive Laura Lindholm, had responded to our tranquillizing treatments. In the morning they would be awakened, informed of their destination, and taken by gur-*sled to the plateau where they would board a* dzo. *It was my duty to check on them. All were sleeping. Music was flowing through all the cabins as well as the sub-brain implants.*

We were never sure if the sleep-indoctrination methods were effective. They had been used by The People for many generations to imbue their own with love for our god and our traditions, but we had no way of knowing if the simpler minds of the world's next civilization could accept or interpret the images.

I slipped into the twilight-lit cabin of the man who would be my mate in the future world. His face, as beautifully innocent as that of Elsbeth or Bakie Bean, was in repose, and I could feel the waves of love and reverence that emanated from him. He found joy in the serene beauties of the natural world, the smell of winter-enriched loam, the merry sound of a brook, the vivid colors of sunset, and the pale tints of dawn. He loved the animals of his world and even pitied the predatory fox that must be caught in a trap. Child laughter aroused a great longing in him, and he dreamed wistfully of the touch of an infant's hand against his cheek. The total innocence and goodness that flowed from him washed over me, leaving me humble and grateful that I had known such a person. I touched my kay *first to his forehead, then to mine, with the fervent prayer that evil might never touch him, that disillusionment should never mar the beauty of his inner being.*

I found it restful to slip momentarily into his warm and simple world. My frets and tensions drained away as I lay beside my sleeping lover, bathing in his calm, drawing strength from his unwavering faith in the ultimate goodness. I discovered, somewhat to my surprise, that I needed him as much as he needed me. I needed the haven he would provide for me, especially whn my thoughts soared too far and scorched wings, and when the burden of my duties bore me down.

At the end of the image-impression broadcast was a vocalized reading by Shur-Et-Na. He had a lilting voice that both soothed and inspired, and though I had heard this speech many times, I paused to savor again the beauty of it.

"It is our hope," he said, spacing his words slowly, "that you will each take to the bestial dark age into which you are going a tiny torch to light your way and that of those around you. To quote one of your nineteenth-century poets:

"Out of the dusk a shadow,
Then a spark;
Out of the cloud a silence,
Then a lark;
Out of the heart a rapture,
Then a pain;
Out of the dead, cold ashes
Life again."[1]

I stepped out into the chill, lavender-streaked dawn. The gur-sleds were drawn up, and slave women were already busy at the oven. The recruits must be awakened soon, given their belongings, and readied for the Time-journey.

Ben-Ad and Gar-Na fell into step beside me. They were dressed in tight-fitting suits for flying and carried their black helmets.

"Ready for another battle with the Blue Belt?" my cousin asked lightly. Then we stopped and crossed glances of sadness. This would be our last chance for a goodbye. We embraced, and our thoughts blurred together.

"There's a time for living, and time for dying, Id-Mar. The world you're going into will be a living death, but somehow, my dear cousin, you must find a way to live. There's work to be done when the next world comes to an end." His cheek brushed mine, and he released me.

Gar-Na's arms went around me, and he read the question in my mind.

"Do not pry, little sister-of-work. There are things we cannot reveal. One day, perhaps, after your work is done where you are going . . ."

His arms tightened around me and his lips touched mine, not as lovers, but as brother and sister.

"The future is longer than our counting system; we

[1] *Evolution*, John Bannister Tabb, 1845-1909.

both face peril, but you are the 'stewardess' I want for—for a mission I might undertake one day."

He released me quickly, and the men strode away in step, their kays *twinkling in the dawn light as they discussed plans for the flight. "One day . . ." I rolled the phrase around on my tongue. To one who navigated the far reaches of galaxy distances and maneuvered a craft through the Blue Belt of Time eternal, those words could signify the fulfillment of our ancestral dream.*

Chapter XIX

The recruits, still under partial hypnosis, accepted their belongings and dressed themselves for travel, as they had been told to do. The awakening process had been started by implants in their subconscious minds while they slept, but their responses varied. The cotton-wool wrapping of their dreams was too comforting to be relinquished easily. Osta had seen reality almost from the first, as had Elsbeth, but they were reluctant to leave the world to which they had become accustomed. Argument had been exhausted. Sulkily and tearfully they sorted and re-sorted bundles in order to get the "most necessary" items crammed into the size and weight limitations Shur-Et-Na had imposed.

"Just like the crooket scales at the airport when we started," Osta grumbled.

"Grandpa Shur is not crooked."

"He's a grown-up man. All men bigger ner a fourteen-year-old are a little bit crooket or they couldn't live yet."

"Women, too, you think, *Grossmutter?*"

"Women are just dumb. Now shut up and talk English."

The girl bent to her work, hiding a very grown-up smile.

Nadine and Roy Hamilton were in a shouting argument when the first *gur*-sled drew up near the courtyard.

"You big stupid ox, it's not the place we came to first!"

"You mooing cow, don't you understand what I've

been telling you all along—you've been taken to the fornicatin' brain laundry!"

"Your brain could stand a little laundering . . ."

Ben-Ad nudged them into the sled.

Brother Smith giggled. "The animals went in two by two. There just went the cow and the ox."

"Goats next," Ben-Ad quipped, and Smith got into the sled.

"Just the same," he called back, shaking a finger at the engineer, "goats—real goats, I mean—are noble animals. All I want is to be home again with mine." He settled back, content with his dream of going home.

For some time Alexander Curry had seen reality, but had shrunk from it. He had no confidence in his senses; what he wanted to be told upon awakening was that he had dreamed it all, that it was only a nightmare of the doom he had so often predicted. He sought the company of Howard McMillan and Laura Lindholm.

They were calm. McMillan was grave, but Laura wore an "I-told-you-so" smirk on her plain face. However, there was no malice in her voice when she greeted Curry.

"I don't believe any of you Cassandras back in our time predicted this."

McMillan answered for Curry. "Of course not," he said dryly. "Secrets of the gods don't leak down to mere mortals."

Curry puzzled over the tone of his friend's speech. It implied a slight contempt for the Project Leaders.

"I never said they were gods," he defended.

"You didn't have to. They themselves have practically shouted it in almost every condescending speech to us mere mortals."

"Bov-No-Urr, perhaps," Curry argued, "but you shouldn't include Shur-Et-Na in your statement."

"He's more subtle," McMillan retorted, "but little better with all his lofty preaching. I'm afraid, Alex, that I haven't been taken in by the extravagant claims the Project Leaders have made about planting Greek gods on Olympus and sending the Sun Goddess to the benighted isles of Ainu—or whatever they were called."

"I've been most amused by their hints that they indoctrinated our great religious leaders and philosophers," Laura supplied.

"Don't forget the little French physician who was brought here and given glimpses of the future so that he became the world's greatest prognosticator . . ."

Curry bridled. "How else can you account for the astounding predictions of the great Nostradamus?"

"I just don't account for them," McMillan returned with a light laugh. "I feel no compulsion to explain all the mysteries of the Universe."

Curry's convictions were always subject to change, depending on the strength of another's argument. In this case, however, he clung to his illusion. "There's no way we can establish facts of the cases they have presented in our subliminal indoctrination courses. Yet it makes sense to me that the gods on Olympus were alien to the Greece whose inhabitants they inspired, and that the Sun Goddess of old Japan was a real but an alien creature. Where could they have come from?"

"From the minds of the groping men who needed them," McMillan answered, as he and Laura obeyed Ben-Ad's nod to get into the first sled.

There was no room for Curry, and he turned to the next one.

Ben-Ad left the remainder of the recruits to choose their own space in the waiting sleds. Vera Simpson pushed in beside Curry, and Ella followed her. Others chose their companions.

Everyone shunned the man who was again dressed in a tight-fitting clerical suit. It had been easy to ignore him while he kept himself caged in his cabin and made only rare appearances in the robes they all wore. In the garb of a priest there was something repugnant about him, however. He made several attempts to take a seat, only to be shoved aside until the three sleds for recruits were filled. He was left standing in miserable loneliness, clutching the black suitcase in one hand and the prayerbook he didn't understand in the other. Y-Stan-Urr, forgotten by her father and overlooked in the bustle of departure, came up to stand beside him. The Project Leaders made places for them in their sled, but ignored them as they carried on a spirited discussion with their *kays*.

The man in priest's cloth smiled timidly at the lonely and unlovely woman beside him, and her dark skin browned with a blush.

Dew sparkled on the gray rock through which the path to the plateau wound, and the breath of the *gurs* billowed whitely into the still air. The sun, bloated and blurred by volcanic ash, sat like a sentient monster on the eastern horizon.

Ella Pozniak swept a hand around the scene. "What a picture to paint!" Carefully, she measured with her hands. "It should be put on canvas just as it is, the red, red sun in the pink and lilac sky, the band of lavender ash blending into the deep blue bowl overhead. And out there on the desert we would show the white chalk lines over which slaves are bending, and over there the border of jungle treetops peeking over the escarpment, their dark green flecked with the brilliance of birds and plumed serpents. Oh, if only I were a true artist!"

"If I were a poet," Curry put in thoughtfully, "I'd write an ode to this beautiful morning in a world soon to die. I'd pen a paean of praise to our hosts of Naz-Co who understand the secrets of the Universe, but who still till their fields with primitive tools and travel on the runners of sleds."

"Wonderful!" Vera Simpson chimed. "The Living Word is here!"

Hugh raised his head from "Tana's" shoulder to ask, "Have we come out of the tunnel yet?"

The young woman laid her *kay* on his forehead. "Soon, very soon, Hugh, my darling."

When the sleds drew up in a cluster in front of a utility cabin on the flying field Robert Smith ran to the panting animals. He fed them morsels he had stuffed into his pockets from the breakfast table, caressing first one, then another. They nuzzled him affectionately, the shadows of heartbreak clouding their large, expressive eyes.

Pretty Bean jounced the whimpering Junie and sang off-key, "Merrily we roll along, roll along . . ."

Osta Eisen silenced her with a look. The young mother put a hand over her mouth.

"Sorry, Osta . . . I mean, Missus Eisen. With children you kind of forget about grown-up mourning." She tried to get out of the sled with the child in her arms, and Osta reached up to take it.

"Maybe it's better we all forget. The little ones are the most important, anyway." She tickled the baby's chin and laughed with her.

The recruits, with the exception of the ostracized priest, drew together as if for mutual protection. None wanted to admit the reality of the bleak, pumice-covered plateau with the weird markings of the Chart trailing off to the vanishing point, and the waiting clamshell craft resting on slim runners. It was not what they remembered as the location where they had landed, and the *dzo* was nothing like the small conventional plane they thought had brought them to a salt flat. Yet because of the process of their awakening, they doubted their memories, not their present vision. Also, they felt strange and slightly embarrassed in their original clothing. Several of the women cooed at the infant, whom Osta kept in her arms. Brock and Joe Quail jockeyed for position to admire Nadine's padded hips encased in bougainvillaea velvet. She had not forgotten how to express herself in movement.

Ella continued to expound on the beauties around them. "Notice the calico-like pattern on the desert formed by the red and blue and white stones. There are birds, calico birds . . ."

"Calico birds in calico trees!" Hamilton snorted. "What's with you double-dyed dopes? Have you all been brainwashed by these Red gooks? Ain't there a damned one of you that's going to raise a howl about where we're being turned loose? Don't you know your rights under the Geneva Agreement? You can make demands. Or—" He lowered his voice conspiratorially and thrust his head into the huddled circle. "—you can listen to me for a change."

They listened. McMillan was especially attentive, as he had been in the sled when Roy spouted his beliefs. There was nothing else to do in the inactive last minutes while Project Leaders and the *dzo* crew conferred inside the cabin.

Hamilton, pleased by the attention he had gotten at last, continued, "Joe Quail has one o' them sticks they use to fly these crates with, and you know me, I'm the guy that put the *fly* in flyboy. I can navigate by the seat o' my pants, too. Now, all of you get ready to pile in, and off we go in our own private chariot. Joe, let's go!"

Somewhat reluctantly. Quail trotted behind Hamilton, who ran toward the waiting *dzo.*

Before anyone quite realized what was taking place, the priest rushed in as swiftly and menacingly as a *zig-tag.* He took a stance, dipped his left shoulder, dived a hand into his clothing, and held something black and sinister in it. The thing coughed and jerked.

Hamilton spun around, clawed the air above him, then fell heavily on his back. His startled eyes looked unblinkingly at the sky, and the ground beneath him reddened.

Nadine shrieked and threw herself across his body.

Joe Quail, with scarcely a heartbeat of hesitation, flipped his *kay* to focus on the killer. The man in priest's garb sank limply to his knees, then collapsed.

Alexander Curry moved over and took the gun from the murderer's slack hand. He tossed it back into the open suitcase among the garments of a priest. Shur-Et-Na, Ben-Ad, and Gar-Na ran up, followed by the lumbering Bov-No-Urr and his ungainly daughter.

Shur-Et-Na revived the stunned killer and demanded, "What happened?"

"He—he—" The man in the clerical suit pointed at the body and struggled with speech. "He do damage to the Flame. All good work be spoiled. I shoot once, I shoot to kill."

"Roy wanted to help us," Nadine sobbed.

Id-Mar-Ok pulled her to her feet. "He was the only man I ever really loved," Nadine went on. "Oh, Tana, you don't know what love is!"

The young woman raised her eyebrows. "Don't I?"

Osta threw a blanket over the dead Hamilton, and Brother Smith knelt on the edge of it and began to pray. Several others knelt, including Ella and Osta, who crossed themselves. McMillan folded his hands and bowed his head. After a moment Laura did likewise.

The Project Leader kept his eyes fixed on the face of the killer, who put up his hands to ward off the probing gaze.

"You think I stupid," the man stammered, "like I don't know nothing that goes on. I smart. I understand the talkings around the table and in the room. I listen, but I don't talk so good. Not long I been in America. I like Flame, and I want he should go on." He pointed a finger like a weapon. "Hamilton, he—"

Shur-Et-Na interrupted him, demanding, "Who are you?"

Again the man covered his face. He trembled in a panic of fright. "They after me, all the big hoodlums of the Syndicate. I just do my work, like I paid to do. I shoot once, I kill Lo-Lo Scala . . ."

"Did you kill a priest?"

"No! No!" the man blubbered. "I would not do that. I just tie him up, like Mumble Toes say. I not hurt him. I only take his clothes, his airplane ticket, and his suitcase. Then Mumble Toes drive me to jetport where the priest was going in Lo-Lo's lavender Caddy. So I get on plane when they call name of Father O'Banion."

"What is your name?" the project leader pressed.

"Call me Skulky. I Herman Ledbetter. I do good work."

"What is your work?"

The killer pointed pridefully at his victim. "I shoot once—"

"I see." Shur-Et-Na consulted silently with his associates, then turned back to the hoodlum. His tone was acid.

"If I could make anyone unborn, it would be you, Herman Ledbetter. There is no suitable place in any time for such as you, but we will not stoop to your level and take your life in payment for the one you have taken here."

Bov-No-Urr shook his *kay* at the murderer. "There's no place for you here. You're not a fit companion for the insane or for the mad killer we're going to capture . . ."

The man in priest's garb lifted a tortured face. "I love Flame, Mister Chief. I want to carry him, make the world good, and build beautiful t'ings."

"You have a lifetime of evil to atone for, Herman Ledbetter," Shur-Et-Na pronounced, "but men and women who have committed the worst of all wrongs against their fellow-beings, as you have done, have found the forgiveness of Oom by humbling themselves completely."

"Do I ask forgiveness for all the men I shooted, or just this one?"

Shur-Et-Na folded his arms and drew himself up regally. "For all of them."

"And do I ask to be forgived for taking money to kill the others?"

"You most certainly do."

Ledbetter, mumbling to himself unintelligibly, closed his eyes, lowered himself to hands and knees, and touched his lips to the stony ground.

The Project Leader assisted him to his feet. "The good that is in you has my blessing, Ledbetter. Now go into the *dimd* and get out of those clothes. Put on some of Hamilton's; he doesn't need them. I am sending you with the others, and I charge you with the responsibility of guarding them from harm."

Ledbetter nodded vigorously. "I do that good, Mister Shurtna. I shoot once, I shoot to kill."

Shur-Et-Na handed him Hamilton's bag. "Where you're going, Ledbetter, your adversaries will use clubs and stones in combat. You are to have no advantage. That will be your punishment, and may you live to save the lives of worthy ones."

He swept up the priest's suitcase, closed it, and handed it to his son. "Drop this and the clothes Ledbetter is wearing into a hole in time. We have no use for a gun here."

Quail, who stood to one side toying with his *kay,* shot a questioning glance at Ben-Ad and received an answer. "Catch," he said, tossing the instrument, which the engineer caught. "I won't have any use for that, either."

Brock leveled a finger at the man who had just entered the cabin. "Don't let that hoodlum get away with murder! Shoot him with his own gun!"

McMillan asked calmly, "Who of us would act as executioner?"

Brock subsided, muttering, and turned to comfort the weeping Nadine.

Shur-Et-Na bowed in mock deference to Dr. McMillan. "Do you wish to organize a tribunal to sit in judgment?"

"We are still under the jurisdiction of your society,

Mister Shur-Et-Na," Curry put in quickly. "I think we all agree you have handled the matter admirably."

"But we don't agree!" McMillan snapped. All eyes turned to him.

He cleared his throat, pulled down his jacket, and wriggled his neck further out of the tight collar—unconscious mannerisms that prepared him to face a class or a congregation.

"Has it occurred to any of you"— he swept his eyes around the huddled group —"that the dead man may have been partially right? He was apparently the only one of us—and I include myself in this—who realized what had happened to us and who resisted the 'brainwashing.' The bald fact is that we were abducted, kidnapped, 'snatched,' and brought to a place of confinement. Our lives were interfered with, and with no more concern than we would have in slaughtering cattle. We were inspected on the hoof, cut out of our herds, given the stun treatment, and driven to market, as it were. We, citizens of a democratic nation of the twentieth century, were given less consideration than we give the cattle we kill for food. Or, as the late Mister Hamilton tried to point out, less consideration than prisoners of war. Irrespective of the 'messages' directed to our subconscious minds while we slept, and all this build-up about 'gods of the future,' we have been and still are prisoners.

"What is worse, in my opinion, is that the captors thwarted the plan of our own God for us. He had prepared a just punishment for the sins we had committed individually and collectively. We were destined to die, all of us and all our kind, in a searing flame of our own creation . . ."

At this point the fury which had been boiling within Bov-No-Urr burst its bounds. He thrust his *kay* like a sword at the speaker. Dr. McMillan paled, clutched his throat, and sank to the ground unconscious.

"Now listen to me!" the choleric Administrator shouted.

No one listened. Instead, contagious anger flared, and the group that had been scoffing and twittering at McMillan suddenly became a small mob to surge forward menacingly. Nadine tensed her hands into claws and reached for Bov-No-Urr's purpling neck. Others picked up stones or handfuls of pebbles.

Y-Stan-Urr leaped like a great cat and bore Nadine to the ground. The mob turned to her and peppered her with small stones and pebbles.

Bov-No-Urr, unnerved, whimpered. "You're sending a useless rebel and a murderer into life, and leaving us here to die like the stupid *gur*-followers of the god Oom!" He regarded the women struggling on the ground. "Kill her, Y-Stan, and take her seat on the *dzo!*"

A club that was a knotted fist on a brawny arm shot out and felled the Project Administrator.

"We have ended the killing, and now we go carry the Flame!"

Herman Ledbetter, dressed in Hamilton's leather breeches and jacket, pushed the limp form of Bov-No-Urr aside and drew Y-Stan to her feet. She blinked up at him, admiring his strength.

"You my kind of woman," he pronounced. "Now on, you fight who I say, when I say." She answered him with a smile.

Shur-Et-Na helped McMillan to his feet. He raised his *kay*.

"There is profound truth in what Doctor McMillan was trying to tell you," he said contritely. "We of Naz-Co have been selfish and blind. So profound has been our belief in our own god and our own traditions that we have failed utterly to see or to understand the development of the human race in a civilization that followed the destruction of our own world. Just as our ancestors of the Precious Blood subjected the animal creatures they found on this planet to stimulation that made them into the human beings we are, we have sought to mold human beings like ourselves into gods so that they, in turn, might shape cultures of the future. With the best of intentions we have erred. Had I understood in my youth what Doctor McMillan has so forcefully brought to my attention, I should not have joined the Projects at Naz-Co. I believe I would have urged the Council of Nobles to abolish them and let the worlds of the future look to their own gods and live and die according to their ways. I do not know how my associates feel about this matter, but for my part I must seek the forgiveness of the god I worship for my own gross error."

Slowly, ceremoniously, he drew his robes around his body and lowered himself to the ground, where he assumed the posture of abasement and touched his lips to the earth.

Gar-Na, Ben-Ad, and Id-Mar-Ok did likewise, while the bewildered Bov-No-Urr looked on. Then, seeing the effect Shur-Et-Na had achieved with the recruits, he followed them.

Dr. McMillan, sitting to one side, stared in surprise at the upraised buttocks of the Project Leaders and the statue-like group of recruits.

Laura, who had been massaging his wrists, put her lips to his ear and whispered, "You missed the best part of the show."

"Must have." He scrambled to his feet. A glance at the awed faces of the recruits told him that the ploy of the Administrator had been successful.

"Oh, no!" He groaned and turned away.

Laura placed an affectionate hand on his shoulder. "You can always say *eeeeee,* you know."

He sighed and made a gesture of resignation. "I suppose I have always enjoyed martyrdom." He squeezed her hand and smiled. "It won't be so bad if you're there to take away the faggots as they're thrown on the fire."

After a dazed moment Hugh rushed to his beloved and helped her to her feet. "There's no need to feel badly, darling Tana. We're out of the tunnel now, and we'll go on in the light. Let's get in the plane and go home."

"Yesth," she said, feigning the lisp she had adopted in their first meeting. She took his arm.

He drew himself up to almost her height and possessively escorted her toward the waiting *dzo.*

Joe Quail picked up Bakie, put a free hand under Pretty Bean's elbow, and followed.

Brock offered an arm to Nadine. "We started out together, Tweety-Tweet."

She walked with him to the *dzo* without a backward glance.

Brother Smith dusted off his knees and giggled. "Two by two," he muttered, and scooped up a handful of soil to drop on the blanket-covered form.

Herman Ledbetter, clutching Y-Stan-Urr's arm, followed Smith's lead and sprinkled a fistful of cinders over the body of his victim.

"I'm sorry Hamilton not go with us. He always lots of fun."

Osta embraced Shur-Et-Na. "Thank you, my *Vater,* for not making me with butterfly ears."

He led his daughter and the sober Elsbeth to the *dzo.* Then he lifted his *kay* to Id-Mar-Ok who was waiting beside the steps.

The Diary

As I crossed kays *with my beloved Project Leader I tried to remember the poem of parting I had learned as a Maiden of Precious Blood. Too much had transpired since that time, and my mind was sodden with heavy memories and unshed tears.*

While we stood with kays *pressed together, smiling to cover the pain that tugged at our throats, a distant rumble like thunder was heard. Soon the earth began to swell into the long waves of a massive tremor. Shur-Et-Na pushed me up the steps. As I hesitated at the entrance a cloudburst of pumice rained down, joining the sky and the earth in hostility toward men. My father-of-work walked away along a white line of the Great Chart. The pudgy Bov-No-Urr loped after him, both going without fear to meet the Doomsday of our world.*

Ben-Ad closed the shell of the dzo *and we lifted toward the Blue Belt of Time to find a day after Doomsday.*

THE END